THE STRAY

THE STRAY

MATTHEW EATON

BUBBA PRESS 2021

First Paperback Edition © Copyright 2021

ISBN
978-1-949381-25-2 Paperback
978-1-949381-26-9 eBook

Bubba Press
PO Box 300
Brownsboro, TX 75756
www.bubbapress.com

Dedicated to my son,
and all those who helped make this possible.

CHAPTER 1

This is not the end. You are bigger than this moment, the voice said in a comforting manner as I lay on the cold tile floor of my bathroom. I had been through that several times before but it never got any easier. I used every bit of strength I could to pull my face up to the toilet, and I vomited for about the eighth time. My face slammed back down against the tile floor.

I started to pray again. I was never much of a praying man, but at times like that...why not. Detox can drive a man insane and make him desperate. Like your whole body being pulled apart by a thousand men from the inside out. I prayed and prayed and gasped, it was so hard to breathe. I could feel fingers running through my cold, wet hair, but I knew it was only a hallucination. But it was still very, very real. I was there alone. I knew I was alone, my eyes were not even open.

I had lain there for hours with my cell phone clutched in my hand, waiting for the text message to let me know the "goods" had come in. I knew it would be any minute, but with every passing second it became harder and harder and I would lose hope. This was not my first time to detox, but this was definitely the worst.

It started with pain pills then it moved up to heavier pain pills, then eventually I caught up with heroin. I always told myself I did it for the pain from the accident, but I knew I could tolerate the pain, the physical pain that is. It's the mental pain that I had a hard time with. My life had definitely not turned out in the way that I hoped it would.

It started about three years ago. I started drinking, and drinking was how it always started.

My two brothers and I were out driving around, having a good time one night, when my oldest brother, Jeff, had way too much to drink (we all had way too much to drink) and he hit a culvert that sent the car flipping in the air. My youngest brother, David, died on impact. Jeff walked away with just a concussion. As for me, I was left with a few broken bones and a lifetime of misery.

As I lay there on the floor that was all I could think about, the accident. How that was the beginning of it all. That day was when my life turned around for the worst. I lost two brothers that day — one in jail for a long time, that I hated, I could not stand to look at him because I saw how much I hated myself when I looked in his eyes. He had been in jail for three years and I'd yet to even visit — and then I lost my other brother forever.

I tried to think soothing thoughts and happy things, but at that point in my life I could not think of anything that made me happy. And yes, I prayed to God, not for him to heal me because I knew he wouldn't, but for him to just let me die there on the floor.

Even though I would go through the process about every six months to a year, I knew I was not near strong enough that time. I knew it was the end. I could feel my organs shutting down. I would gasp for air but couldn't get any. It was definitely the end. In a way I was relieved. I just hoped it would come sooner so I wouldn't have to lie on the floor any longer.

I tried to stand up, but I stumbled down. There was just no motivation for me to do anything. I needed water, Gatorade or something, something to make it go away. What I wouldn't give for ten minutes of clarity and without pain. My guts were wrenching inside. I'd scream out every now and again, but I knew this pain wouldn't end. I knew no matter what I did or what I said this wasn't going to end and this was my entire fault. I put myself in that position.

It had been three years now since I have been addicted to drugs. Going through detox was the hardest thing I had ever been through. You'd never feel so alone as when you were going through something like that. No matter how many people you had in front of you, you just couldn't seem to feel any better. There was only one way to feel better and that was to get high. That was why I wouldn't let go of my phone, my friend would call any minute to let me know the drugs were in and then I would be good.

I decided after this time I was going to ease off the heroin. It was too much. The detox was so bad. The pills I could handle. Too many times I clutched a pistol in my hand, coming real close to ending it. If only they could see me now, all the people in my life that I hide it from. All the acquaintances, the loved ones, but who am I kidding, I don't have many of those.

I owned a small furniture shop in town and the only people I had anything to do with were the people who paid me to build furniture for them. What killed me the most was one of my customers I knew I could call and they would have some Vicodin, or some pills or something, to make it better. But that was a line I couldn't cross, letting someone know about the demons I had inside of me, about who I really was, in a town this small. It would be out. It already was out, but the few people who didn't know were the ones I wouldn't want to know. I was already struggling with my business as it was. I could definitely lose the business doing something like that.

So, there I was again, once again on the floor, dying inside and praying to God to let me die. It was becoming an all-too-familiar feeling.

I tried to struggle to get up once more. Once again, I could hear the voice whispering in my ear, telling me everything would be okay. I was sure it was my imagination making it up, but for a brief moment it felt like I was not alone anymore.

When I got to my knees, the phone rang and I answered it. It was him. He told me to meet him outside, he was ten minutes away.

I had more strength than I ever had in that next thirty seconds because I knew it was only minutes before this hell, this living hell, would be over.

I got to my feet, eyes still closed because I could not open them, it was too bright. I ran outside. As I did, I tripped when I ran out into the yard and he showed up shortly after.

I swore from that day on, I would never put myself in that position again.

CHAPTER 2

I woke up to the alarm clock blaring, which felt like the hundredth time, but I knew it wasn't. I hit the snooze button at least two times already, so I knew it was time to get up. I sat up on my bed and rubbed my face and instantly felt angry. The mornings were never a good time for me. I was always sore. My shoulders and my knees always hurt, so I sat up on my bed and just rubbed my face, knowing I was going up against a day I was not looking forward to. But these days that was not uncommon.

I had once read an article on how you treat your mornings is how the rest of the day will treat you. Well, if that was true, I knew I was screwed every day.

I got up, carefully limped to the coffee pot and turned it on, walked over to the sink and splashed water over my face trying to wake myself up. I always woke up late. I never had time to do much, and I dreaded that look in the mirror every morning because I hated what I saw. I hated what I had become. Just seeing myself in the mirror was a constant reminder of the things I never did, but at this point in my life apathy had become a comforting reminder.

I jumped in the shower. It was always hot. It always relaxed me and made me feel a little bit better. As I stumbled out of the shower, I glanced in the mirror one time and realized I was about a month overdue for a haircut and hadn't shaved for a couple of weeks. My appearance was never very important to me. My long brown hair and my increasingly-growing thick beard may have looked bad but it matched how I felt on a daily basis. I knew I was going to have a hard time finding clean clothes because doing laundry was one of the things I hated most. I would wait until it was absolutely necessary before I wasted half a day washing clothes just so I could get them dirty again. I picked up clothes off of the floor, smelling them until I found something that didn't smell too bad.

As I threw on jeans and a shirt I looked around the house, making sure I was not forgetting anything. This house was still new to me. I had only been living in it for a few months. It once belonged to my grandmother who had passed about a year ago. I think she left it to me because she wanted to know I would always have a place to stay. The house was about sixty years old. It was a white frame house that my grandfather had built when they were married.

Now, the house was falling apart and probably should have been burned to the ground, but I just couldn't do that. My grandmother was one of the few people in my life that truly loved me unconditionally. No matter what the problems I was facing in life, I could walk through her door and everything would be okay. I never knew my grandfather because he had died before I was born. I do know that he picked the perfect women to spend the rest of his life with even though it was a short one.

I poured a very large cup of coffee and walked out the door. I started my car up, which was a surprise because it didn't start about half the time. It was a 1970 Chevelle that I had since high school. It wasn't in horrible shape. It was painted black and had black interior. It all needed to be redone. I'd always planned to fix it up when I became an adult; would have money and time and all these things then I would fix the car up and it would be nice, but none of that ever came. I was still a twenty-seven-year-old child.

I owned a furniture shop there in town, and I could barely pay the bills. About once a month I wouldn't even take a check home, because there was nothing to take home. I only lived a few miles from my shop, but it always took me about twenty minutes to get to work because I never went straight there. I had to drive around and take the long way just so I could get my shit together. I would take a couple of back roads, smoke a couple of cigarettes and finish my coffee before I got to work. I was always twenty minutes late, but that was okay because my best friend since high school, Ellis, always seemed to get there on time and was on top of everything. He has always followed me around since high school. I think Ellis knew that if he didn't look after me that no one would. It could be that his long beard and tattoo-covered arms made it impossible for him to get a job anywhere else. He was a good guy, always there for me. You could not ask for more in a best friend. He was more like a brother. He took care of the day-to-day things in the furniture shop when it took me about four hours every morning just to wake up and get ready for the day.

I rode into Juniper, a small town in eastern Texas, the same place I was born and raised and grew up. It was exactly like the kind of town you would see on a television show from the 60s. There were about four thousand people in the town and everyone knew everyone. Everyone got their hair cut at the same place; they got it cut at Jane's Barber Shop on Main Street. If you stopped at a gas station every morning you would see the same people. It was a friendly enough town and I loved it, but I hated it just as much. Every morning once I would drive into town the sun would rise in the same spot and it was just the monotony every day. Driving into this town was a constant reminder of what my everyday life had become.

I pulled up to the shop. It wasn't much to look at but it was all I could afford. The building I owned used to be a gas station. I bought it and slowly turned it into my furniture shop. The pumps still stood outside and occasionally someone passing through town would pull up to them thinking I would run outside and fill their car up with gas. The first time it happened Ellis pretended to pump their vehicle with gas and he actually cleaned their windshield. We laughed about that for days, maybe even weeks. Ellis was always fun to work with and I never had to wonder if he had my back.

As I pulled up I noticed Ellis was already there, as I had figured. I went straight into my office trying to avoid him because every morning he had a list of things we had to do that day or things to expect, and I just did not want to hear it. I instantly went to my office, walked to my desk and sat down. As I looked there was a pile of envelopes on my desk that said Tyler Hagen on it, which was me, and it was bills, past due, stuff I could not pay. Either that or I could not give Ellis a paycheck, which I would die before that happened. So, I flipped through the bills and threw them to the side. About that time Ellis popped his head in and told me not to forget Ms. Evans was coming by to look at her dining room suite, which was not bad news. We were done with that, been done with it for two weeks, and I could use the payday, but I needed more money. I called Ellis back into my office and explained to him that we needed to make some side money. We needed to do something, we were in trouble.

I had done this several times before. Anything from drugs to anything we could make a profit on. I even did a little mechanic work on the side if I needed to, or hang sheetrock or do whatever. But the best money was in the drugs and when I told Ellis we needed to make more money he knew what I was talking about. It was one of those unspoken things we had. He told me he would look into it. I told him thanks.

The day went by pretty slow. I spend most of the day in the office when I should have been in the shop helping with the furniture, but it had gotten to a point where helping with furniture was just something I didn't care to do. It was springtime, so it was not too hot yet in Texas. It would get up to about seventy-five to eighty during the day, which was great weather, but still being outside, being hungover, it just was not happening.

I looked at the clock. It was about noon, so I reached in my desk drawer and pulled out a handful of Vicodin, about four, and swallowed them with a shot of vodka. I know everybody says you cannot smell vodka, that is why I started drinking it, but you can smell vodka. So, I told myself it was for the pain just to get through the day. I mean it was noon. That was one thing I was always good at, I always felt guilty about drinking or taking any kind of narcotics before noon, but I am telling you I would count the hours until noon.

When I realized it was about lunchtime, I was fixing to head out and saw a Suburban pull up. I looked out the window and that is when I saw her get out. It was Anna Stephens.

Anna Stephens was the only proof to me that there was a God. I had known her for about ten years. She was beautiful. Perfect. It was almost as if when she walked you could see a glow. You could honestly see a glow. My heart sank and my stomach tied up in knots every time I saw her. I was in love with her. I had been in love with her since the day I saw her. We went out a few times. I always kept in touch with her, but she got married and started a family. She had a daughter, so I never really had my chance, or at least that is what I told myself.

I didn't know why she was stopping by. Anna had long dark hair and green eyes. She was the most beautiful girl in town and she didn't even know it. Anytime I tried to tell her how beautiful she was, she would blush and quickly change the subject. She was raised in Juniper, too. She became very religious after high school. I never knew why she ever had anything to do with me. I always figured she would realize that she was way better than me and move on. That never happened though. She would stop by occasionally just to talk, tell me how things were going.

Today she walked in with a big smile on her face, as I had on mine. She gave me a big hug and asked how I was doing. I always had a big smile when I saw her. I lied and told her everything was great. I asked how she was.

"Doing good," she said.

We talked for about thirty minutes. I offered to take her to lunch, but she said she had other things she had to do. But I knew she didn't. In a town this small she couldn't be seen having lunch with me. Her husband may work out of town, but he would be getting a text message before we got through eating. That was understandable. I didn't want to get her into any kind of trouble. I loved her. I just wanted her to be happy.

I still remember the day someone told me she was getting married. I had flashes through my head of stopping the wedding and she would fall in love with me then we'd live happily ever after. Of course, I never had the courage to do it or tell her, and I don't think any woman would live happily ever after with me.

I often wondered if maybe we had been in a relationship then maybe the accident would've never happened. If maybe my brother would still be alive. Or if maybe somehow my life would be great. But I couldn't think that way; it was a waste of time. I was in this life forever. I was never going to make a lot of money, I was always going to be addicted to drugs and I would constantly wonder about life and the decisions I'd made.

After she left I was somewhat motivated to work a little. So I went out to the shop and talked to Ellis. We went over a few things, a few projects we were working on, kind of made a schedule for the week about what we were going to do. After that I went back into my office. I couldn't get Anna off my mind. It was like that. I wouldn't see her for a few days, maybe even a week, but once I would run into her or she would text me after that it would take me a day or two just to get her off my mind.

Once I knew I couldn't get her off my mind I had to find a substitute. So, I got my cell phone out and texted Lady.

Lady had been a friend of mine for about a year now. She worked about thirty miles out of town at a strip club. Beautiful girl, maybe not the kind of girl you marry, but definitely the kind you waste some nights with to ease your suffering from someone else. I texted her and asked her if she would be around because I didn't want to go home to a lonely house. Just the thought of Anna sitting down and having dinner with her husband and laying in bed together would kill me. So I had to make it a late night tonight. I knew how it would end, too. I would lose a couple hundred dollars at the strip club. Of course, I would have to tip Lady to get her to come home with me. Her real name was Annette or something similar to that but I always called her Lady, I wanted to keep things simple.

The day had actually gone by quick. I only had a couple of things to do before I could head home and take a shower and head up there. I decided to get my work done as fast as I could so I could head over to my folks house and check in on them. It had been a couple of weeks since I had seen them. So I went to the back and helped Ellis for about an hour then told him I had to leave. My parents lived about thirty minutes out of town in the opposite direction so that would kill a little bit of time. I figured I could spend a little bit of time with them, head home, shower and it would be time for me to head up to the strip club.

I had a nice thirty-minute drive and random thoughts would go through my head as the music would blare. Thoughts of Anna went through my brain constantly. I pulled in the driveway and there it sat, just the way it sat for the last thirty years. It was an old log cabin they lived in.

I walked inside to find my mom cleaning and my father out back on the tractor. I gave mom a big hug and told her it was good to see her. She asked how things had been, and of course I would lie to her and tell her everything was going fine, that business was doing good. She offered me a glass of sweet tea. I sat and talked to her for a good thirty minutes. I wanted to spend enough time there so I wouldn't feel guilty about not staying long enough, but I also wanted to get out of there before my father got off the tractor. I did love my father, but as hard-headed as he was, we couldn't actually have a relationship. He was a bitter, tired, broken man. He hated to see anybody accomplish anything that was possibly better than what he did in life.

I had a casual conversation with my mother talking about the business, life, and of course she told me some gossip about a lady at her church. I pretended to care, but I really didn't. I just wanted to spend some time with her then I could get out of there. It would buy me at least another week or two before I would have to stop back by. As time was passing, I thought I was going to make it, but right about that time my father walked in as I was sitting at the table talking to my mom. He walked right past me and didn't even say a word, which was normal for him. He didn't care that I had stopped by. I was just a reminder to him about the two sons he had lost, and since we had never seen eye-to-eye, it isn't like he could ever have a relationship with me. His favorite was always my younger brother David, the one who died in the accident. He never blamed me for the accident because I was not driving, but he did blame me because I was there and did nothing.

Our conversations were short. He would always ask me about the business and how it was doing with a smirk on his face like he knew I was struggling. He probably heard from somebody in town about how bad I was doing and wanted to rub it in my face. That was fine. After twenty-seven years you get used to it. I would say hi, ask him how it was going, then I would leave before I gave him an opportunity to say anything. I gave my mom a hug goodbye, told her it was good to see her.

By this time it was starting to get dark, so I knew it was time to go. I got into my car and started it up with a sigh of relief that I didn't have to have a conversation with my father.

CHAPTER 3

I pulled up to my house, walked in and put my keys on the table and jumped in the shower. I never liked going to the strip club without being clean. It didn't take long, I jumped out of the shower, threw on a new t-shirt, a spray of some cologne and I was out the door.

As I pulled to the end of my driveway I stopped for a minute, trying to decide if I was making the right decision going to the strip club. It was the middle of the week and I needed to be up early, but I sat there with my car idling and the radio on. I looked in my rearview and saw my house, and realized that if I didn't go it would just be a long, miserable night by myself, and that just wasn't going to happen. I opened my glove compartment, pulled out a pill bottle and emptied about five Vicodin in my hand, and took them with a swig of a drink I had mixed before I left. I knew by the time I pulled up to the strip club they would be kicking in and I would be feeling great about my decision.

It was about a twenty-minute drive to the strip club, a drive I really did not mind. I think half the reason I'd go was for the drive. I could turn the radio on, I could think…could think about everything.

As I was heading towards the strip club, I began to think about the business, and about Anna. I couldn't get her off my mind. Running into her was the main reason I was going up there. It's bittersweet every time I see her. I got to be with her and spend time with her, but I also got the constant reminder of what I wanted but could never have. I rolled the windows down. It was about seventy-five degrees. I turned the radio up as loud as I could. The twenty-minute drive normally felt like ten. I always loved the smell this time of year, that's why I would roll the windows down with spring coming. You could smell the asphalt from the heat of the day, could smell fresh-cut grass.

It was mostly highway to the strip club. The club was located about twenty miles out of Juniper, and if you go about fifteen miles further you go into the city. I think that is where the club got most of its business, from the city. I usually went there about two to three times a month. I have yet to run into anybody I know from Juniper. Juniper was the kind of town where if you ran into someone you knew at the club, strip club at least, people began to talk and most people were not willing to take that risk. Of course, I didn't care.

It made me wonder about Anna stopping by today. For some reason it almost seemed like she would plan it just right. I may not see her for a week or two before she crossed my path again. It was like she didn't want me to forget she was still there. Of course, I read too much into everything. It was probably coincidence.

My phone rang; it was Ellis. He called wanting me to go have a beer with him. I tried to talk him into coming up to the strip club, but he wouldn't do that. He was also one of those that were afraid people would see him. Plus if his girlfriend found out he was with me at the strip club that probably wouldn't be a good thing for him or their relationship.

I got off the phone about the time I was pulling into the strip club parking lot. It was weird. People were not from around here and when I pulled up to it you really began to wonder how this club could be here right in the middle of nowhere. There were a couple gas stations that were not far, but other than that this club was the only thing nearby. I am sure it had something to do with city ordinances as the reason why they were so far out, but they still got plenty of business. They probably got more business from being out of town because people were more likely to stop by and park in the back.

It was a big building, two stories tall. Being a weeknight it wasn't too busy. As I pulled into the back, I could see there were only about a dozen cars. I was a little relieved to see there weren't many people there. When this place was crowded it could get pretty ridiculous. I've been coming here enough I knew all the bouncers and even the girls. Most of the girls wouldn't stay long working in a place like this for more than six-to-eight months, but a few of them had been there a while.

As I walked through the door up to the front counter to pay the ten-dollar cover charge, the girl up front just nodded her head and told me to go ahead and go on back. That was one of the perks for being a regular, I guess. As I walked through the hallway and opened up the curtain to the main stage, the music was loud and the girls were dancing. At first glance I didn't see anybody I recognized. There were a handful of people that looked like some kind of bachelor party or something going on in the corner, but most of the tables were empty. One of the bouncers came up to me and asked me where I would like to sit. I motioned to the corner and as I did I lit up a cigarette. The waitress saw me and immediately headed towards me and asked me what I wanted to drink. I ordered a beer and a shot and sat down.

At first glance I didn't see her. I sat there for about ten minutes, drank half my beer and had another shot before Lady walked in and I saw her across the way. She smiled like she was excited to see me, but with strippers you never knew if they were telling the truth or not. She was beautiful. She was by far the most beautiful girl there and had been, and I think the only reason she had worked there for over a year is because being the most beautiful girl at a strip club had its advantages. She probably made fifty-grand a year dancing naked. Who could blame her?

She walked towards me. I caught myself with a half grin on my face. I realized I was actually kind of excited to see her. It had been a few weeks since I had seen her. Normally I didn't go this long.

Her stage name was Lady. Her real name was Annette, but I never used her real name, I guess I liked Lady better. She sat down beside me, gave me a kiss on the cheek.

"How you doing," she asked.

"Good. How've you been?"

"Oh you know, just working hard."

I grinned a little and said, "I bet."

She pulled something out of her bra and handed it to me. I could feel without even looking, it was about ten Vicodin. I didn't count them. Just handed her a few twenties and told her I appreciated it.

"Is that all you came for tonight?"

I looked in her eyes. "Well, that is half the reason I came."

She smiled. "Well I'm going on stage in a minute. When I get through I'll come back and we'll talk."

"That's fine." I needed some time apart from her. I could take a couple more Vicodin and a couple more shots. A waitress came over with a drink I didn't order, and she could tell I had a puzzled look on my face.

"It's on the house," she said. "It's from Bobby."

Bobby was the owner. I had been a regular for a couple years, so I got to know him pretty well. He was at the corner of the bar. I took the drink and gave him a slight wave and a nod. He did this from time to time. He was making plenty of money, a single drink wasn't going to hurt. I had actually made some furniture for him about six months earlier, and of course I was drunk when I quoted the price, so I did lose some money on the deal, and I think he knew that. So that is why I got an occasional free drink.

I watched Lady get on stage and watched her dance. She danced to an old Def Leppard song. It was such a cliché, and of course almost every guy in the room went up there to give her a dollar on stage. Going up to the stage was for suckers. You didn't get any personal attention and to be honest with you, it was a little too embarrassing for my taste, having twenty guys stare at you while a girl dances naked in your face and you give her a dollar, even for me was a little too pathetic.

After going from stage to stage for about forty-five minutes, she came back by my table. She sat and we talked, and then of course, I had to get a couple of lap dances because she had to make her money. Even though we were close, I still paid her. Of course, I overpaid. It was worth it. I came up for two reasons — one was to get drunk and the other was to take her home with me.

The night was still early and I had already drank too much. Between the alcohol and the pills, I should've been at home. I already had wasted too much money. I was too drunk to drive, but I was going to drive anyway. You'd think that when your brother dies from a drinking and driving accident it would change the way you do things, but not me. I was too hard-headed. Maybe I just didn't give a shit. Probably both.

We sat there and talked, but something was different. It was almost as if Lady had an agenda. Normally it was a fake conversation, but tonight she was asking me all these questions. She genuinely wanted to know how things were going in my life, which was weird to me, but I played along. I was drunk, so I was honest.

"Why are you here tonight?"

"You know why I'm here."

"I know you come up here every few weeks, and we talk and then we have fun, but we really don't even know each other, even though we have been doing it for eight months now."

I sat up in my chair. After she had said that I was starting to feel uncomfortable. She had questions to answers I didn't have. Then, she looked me straight in the eye and said "Well, what do you want?"

I shook my head out of frustration. The whole point of me coming up there was so I wouldn't have to deal with any of this. I used her as a temporary relief from my daily bullshit, and now she was acting like that wasn't going to be an option anymore.

"Why are you asking me all these questions?" I asked.

"Well, maybe I just want to know where we stand."

"I don't know. I enjoy coming up here. I enjoy spending time with you, and don't forget I pay you for your company."

I knew instantly I had said something I shouldn't have said.

She got pissed. I could see it in her eyes.

"Don't worry, I'll never forget. I'll be back." She got up and walked away.

Now, I just did the one thing I did not want to do. I complicated the one thing in my life that was never complicated.

By this time I decided to have another drink, when I already had about three too many. I walked up to the bar, ordered another drink and sat down. I began to wonder in my drunken state if this wasn't a bad idea. I sat at the bar and had a couple more drinks, and as I saw her walk by I grabbed her by the arm.

"Listen, I come up here because I enjoy spending time with you. I come up here because I want to be with you. It has nothing to do with the pills, the drinking or the good time. I'm in no state to answer any of these questions. Why don't you go get your things ready, it's about closing time."

She looked at me like she had more to say, but I think she knew that right now was not the time to say it. She went and grabbed her stuff and we left. She rode with me. I was way too drunk to be driving, but we made it, and of course there was no real conversation on the way home, just the radio turned up, a lot of smiling and kissing.

We stumbled through the front door, laughing and tripping over ourselves. We both had way too much to drink. I threw her on the bed and we began to kiss, and for a short, very short period of time between being drunk and having her in my arms, it seemed like life froze for a minute. I was not thinking about Anna.

THE STRAY

I was not thinking about the shop or even about the next day. I was just enjoying myself with her.

CHAPTER 4

I woke up the next morning with my head pounding, feeling like my body had gone through a grinder. I rubbed my eyes and slightly leaned up in the bed. I glanced over next to me and saw Lady, she was still asleep. I lay there, still trying to collect my thoughts from the night before, only remembering a small percentage of them. I instantly felt remorse and regret. I knew I'd made some bad decisions, I just wasn't exactly sure what they were.

I sat in bed, thinking. I looked beside me and watching her sleep for a small second there, a short second there, I think I could be happy this way. She was beautiful when she slept. She looked peaceful, and for a second I completely forgot who she was, what kind of person she could be, just watching her sleep. I rolled over and got out of bed, instantly feeling the pain in my knees and my shoulder, I made my way to the counter and poured myself a drink and opened up my pill bottle and got a couple of Vicodin out. I knew in about thirty minutes I'd feel great. I sat down on the couch and noticed what time it was—I was late—but when you feel this bad, being late doesn't really matter.

Then, I heard a knock on the door. First I thought it was Ellis maybe stopping by. It was about the time for him to be driving by, but I could not think of why he would stop by. I got up and walked to the door and opened it. To my surprise, it was Anna. I wasn't even dressed yet. I had a pair of shorts on and that was it. As I opened the door she was looking at me with a very concerned look on her face.

"Hey," I said, surprised.

She hesitated for a second as if I was supposed to say something else, then just stared for what felt like a lifetime, and finally she uttered the words "Are you okay?"

"Yeah, I'm fine. Why?"

She sighed and then looked to her side. I leaned my head out the door and I could see that my car was in the middle of my driveway and my mailbox was laying in the yard.

"Shit." I rubbed my face trying to remember what happened, but I knew whatever thought came to mind wouldn't be one I would want to remember anyway. "Yeah, I'm fine. I had a few drinks last night, that's all."

That disapproving look on her face was new. I knew she cared and I knew deep down that she was probably disappointed in me, but I had never seen it on her face, not like this.

"What is going on with you? These past few weeks—"

I stopped her in the middle of her sentence. "Hey look, Anna, everything is fine. You know, things just got a little crazy last night, then one thing lead to another…" About that time, I heard a cough and could hear Lady getting out of bed. Anna heard it, too.

She walked down the hall and asked "Hey baby, is everything okay?" as she poked her head around the corner.

"Yeah, it's fine, it's fine." When I turned around and looked at Anna, it looked like she had seen a ghost, which I thought was odd. I don't know, maybe since she had never seen me date anyone else she just assumed I didn't have other people in my life.

31

"Go back to bed, I'll be there in a minute." Lady walked back down the hall into the room and I could hear her lay back down. I turned to Anna. "Really, nothing is wrong. I just had a late night."

Anna didn't say much, but the expression on her face and the way she looked at me said more than she could ever say with words. It was instant disapproval. She was very disappointed, I could tell.

Finally, she said, "Hey listen, I've got to run into town for a couple of errands. Why don't you give me about an hour and meet me at the cafe and we'll have a cup of coffee. There are a few things I want to talk to you about."

I looked at her in disbelief because she never wanted to spend much time together, at least not in the middle of town where people could see. I asked her if everything was okay, and she assured me it was, she just wanted to talk to me. So I agreed to meet her there.

I shut the door and actually went and got in the shower, hoping that would make me feel better. Between that and the Vicodin I was sure it would. While I was in the shower the only thing I could think about was what she could possibly want to talk to me about. We were pretty close, but we didn't have that kind of relationship. We didn't share things with each other, not like that, and for her to want to meet and have coffee, it must be something important to her. In the back of my mind I fantasized about her telling me she was getting a divorce, and then maybe my life could change for the best. The more I thought about it, that would be more of a stress on me, constantly pining after her wanting to make her happy, but I knew I never could, especially after the look she gave me this morning. There was no way she could ever see me as anything more than a small-town screw-up.

After the shower I got dressed and walked in to see Lady. She was still in bed. She wasn't asleep, but she had her eyes closed. I walked over and gave her a kiss on the forehead. I told her I had to go to work.

"Work, huh, is that really where you're going?"

"Yeah." I turned around and walked away. I guess she had heard me talking to Anna. She had a grin on her face when she said it, almost as if she was telling me *I know where you're going.* The things she did and what I did when we weren't together didn't matter. If we were together I wouldn't have to give her so much money to spend time with me. So, the comment didn't bother me much.

I walked out of the house, got into my car and headed towards the cafe. I had to pass by my shop in order to get there. I could see Ellis standing outside, I just gave him a wave, and about two seconds later I got a text from him, so I assumed he was wondering where I was headed. I didn't even look at the text. All I could think about was what Anna could possibly want to talk to me about.

As I pulled up to the cafe, I parked at the end of the lot. I walked through the door and instantly said hi to a few people. A town this small, you knew half the people in there. I had some casual small talk, then walked my way to the back. I could see Anna sitting there drinking coffee.

As I walked towards her, I could feel butterflies in my stomach, but I couldn't understand why. The more and more I thought about it, the more convinced I became there was nothing she could possibly say to me that would impact my life one way or another. It's not like she was getting married again. The day she told me she was getting married was a hard day for me. I remember sitting in my truck trying to decide what to do, as if there was anything I could do. I wasn't near the person I needed to be for her, so I spent hours in my truck drinking, trying to come up with some sort of way to feel better about the situation.

I sat down in the chair across from Anna, and the waitress came over. I ordered a cup of coffee, and I could tell Anna had something on her mind because of the way she was playing with her coffee cup. She would cup it in her hands and take her two thumbs and move them around the edge of the lip. She always did that when she was nervous or upset.

After a moment of silence and sitting there, I got my cup of coffee. "Okay, Anna, what's the deal? Is everything okay?"

She looked at me with a very sad grin on her face. "Everything is fine with me," she said. "But what's going on with you?"

I got a little irritated at first because we had just had this same conversation earlier that morning.

"Everything is fine," I said. "Everything is the same as it has always been with me. What's going with you?"

She kind of shook her head. "Everything is the same, huh? You've been acting strange. You know, I stopped by a couple of weeks ago at your shop. Ellis told me you hadn't been showing up to work on time, even missing entire days. Even he was worried about you."

"Anna, is this the reason you wanted to meet with me this morning?" I was a little confused because at no point in our relationship had she ever shown that amount of concern.

"Well, yes. Your mom called the other day to invite me over for your dad's birthday."

I leaned back in my chair and let out a sigh because I could only imagine what her and my mother talked about. I have known Anna long enough that when we were kids, her and my mother had somewhat of a rapport, and to this day they still talked. My mother was the closest thing Anna ever had to a mother.

"What did she say?"

"Well, she's just a little worried about you, too."

"Well, there's no need to be worried about me, everything is fine. Business is fine, my life is fine. I know you saw the mailbox. Sure, I had a few too many drinks, shouldn't have driven home, but it's not the end of the world. Not a big deal."

"Then why don't you ever talk to your father?"

"I do talk to my father, just not very much. You have to understand we don't see things...we just don't see eye-to-eye. Plus, he's kind of an asshole."

She just looked at me like that was the reaction she was expecting.

"Anna, will you tell me what is really going on? Don't get me wrong, I appreciate the concern."

"Well, when I drive by and see your mailbox in your yard, obviously driven over, and I've had conversations with your mother..."

"Come on, Anna, this is not why you wanted to meet with me. What's really going on?"

I could tell by the look in her eyes she was mere seconds away from telling me, it was on the tip of her tongue. There was obviously something else bothering her, but she just sat there. I knew there was more to the story but she wouldn't say it.

"Is everything alright at home?" I asked. She answered yes but in an angry tone. I decided to change the subject. "What errands did you have to run this morning?"

She kind of grinned and shook her head, because she knew that was what I was trying to do, and the whole time we talked she would keep her head down and stared at her coffee cup, rubbing her thumbs along the edge. I'd known her for years and this was one of the weirdest, most awkward conversations we'd ever had. I knew there was more to the story. I just didn't know what it was. She wouldn't answer my question because she knew it was irrelevant. She kept staring down at the coffee cup. We sat there in silence for what felt like an eternity, but it was actually only a few minutes. I was getting a little frustrated. The Vicodin had kicked in and I was starting to feel a better. My whole body started to feel better. I leaned over in the booth and grabbed her hand. She stopped and looked me in the eyes.

"Anna, tell me what is really bothering you."

She quickly removed her hand and sat up straight in the booth, looking around to make sure nobody saw. I instantly felt bad for doing that. She got out of the booth and stood up, grabbed her jacket and her purse. "You've got enough going on, don't worry about it," she said as she left.

I sat there in the booth for a little while longer. I knew I had work to do, I had stuff to do that day, but I was trying to remember what had happened the night before and I was trying to understand what had just happened here.

Since Anna had gotten married we had never spent time like that together. I've never seen her act so troubled, and I believe that part of it was because of my actions. I did believe she cared, but I knew that part of it had to be something else, and there was only one thing I could think of that she would want to tell me but wouldn't tell me: problems at home with her husband. But it was hard for me to imagine she would have problems at home with her husband. As much as I hated the man because he married the woman I loved, he was one of the greatest guys I had ever met. He was nice. He would do anything for anybody and he always provided for her and took care of her and their daughter.

I took a final drink of my coffee and decided to go. It was time to head to work.

CHAPTER 5

I pulled up to the shop and shut my engine off. I didn't get out right away. I sat back in the seat going over what just happened in my head. After having coffee with Anna I still couldn't put the pieces together. None of it made sense. I glanced over and saw Ellis looking at me with his hands up in the air, pointing at his wrist. I was well over an hour late and he knew it. I got out of the car and walked over to him.

"Hey man, we've got to be over at Ms. Evans' place to deliver her furniture in half an hour."

I kind of scratched my head and asked "Is it loaded?"

"Yeah, it's loaded, but it's going to take us about half an hour to get there."

The way I was feeling this morning, and after everything that happened, the last thing I wanted to do was go on a delivery run with Ellis, but I knew I needed to. It was a big payday for us and we needed the money. So, we got in the truck and started heading that way.

"Is everything set for tonight?" I asked Ellis.

"We're going to meet them tonight about eight on Oil Highway, just outside town by the oil derricks."

"That's good."

"They have four AK-47s we can buy for two grand. I've already got a buyer lined up and we can get rid of them the next day for about five hundred in profit."

"All right. You do know these guys, right?"

"Yeah, yeah, of course I do."

I looked at him. I could tell he was hesitant on what to say. "What do you mean? Do you know them or not?"

"Well, I don't know 'em, I know *of* 'em."

Shit, I thought to myself. "Well, can we trust these guys or not?"

"Yeah, yeah, we can trust 'em. Man, I set this up. It is easy money, in and out."

"Alright, if you say so."

The drive felt a lot longer than thirty minutes. The air-conditioner didn't work so I had the window rolled down. I started to sweat, then realized I left my pills in my car. I was low on pills and I didn't know anybody at the time who had any. I always did that shit to myself. I would always let myself get low, not pay attention. There was no telling how many I took last night. My head was still hurting, but not as bad since the pills had kicked in from earlier, and I knew after I did all the heavy lifting with the furniture and sweating I would want a few more, but I would have to wait for the long drive back to get them.

We pulled up into the long driveway of Ms. Evans' house. I didn't even know her first name. I always called her Ms. Evans because she was my seventh-grade algebra teacher. When we got there I realized she evidently made more money than the average teacher...her husband must have been loaded. The house was a huge brick home that couldn't have been more than a few years old.

As we parked, Ms. Evans greeted us in the yard. She did a once over on the furniture to make sure it was everything she wanted. She smiled and let us in. She could have gotten this furniture cheaper from somewhere else, but I think she had us do it just because we had known each other for so long. As we got the furniture in, we put it all together and set it up in her house. It took a few hours. Afterwards, she gave me the check and I thanked her and put it in my pocket. I did not even look at it, but I knew it would be right. I thanked her again, gave her a big hug and told her if she needed anything to give me a call.

Back on the road, I told Ellis I wasn't going to stick around since we were going to be working that night. Had to go home to take care of a few things, and by the bank to get some cash for the deal this evening.

When we got back to the shop I jumped in my car, started it up and quickly grabbed my pills out of the glove compartment. I checked my stash. Enough for a day, maybe two. I knew I was going to be screwed. I instantly felt like an anxiety attack was coming on. This would happen every now and then, when I felt like I was going to run out of pills, and nine out of ten times something always came up where I didn't run out, but still I would get anxiety, a fear, of not having them. A fear of going through withdrawal. I pulled out my phone and sent a few texts to a few different people to see what they had and see what they could come up with. I didn't text Lady because I knew she didn't get them very often, and I'd gotten some from her the night before. Maybe if I hadn't been so careless with them I wouldn't be in this situation, I thought to myself.

I drove to the bank and walked in. There were two banks in town, both of them were full of people I knew. I hated banking there, but it wasn't worth driving thirty minutes to another town. At any point, the tellers could look and see how much money you had in your bank account, and I am sure they did. I walked up to the first teller. Her name was Amy. She graduated a couple years after me, and she had worked at this bank for about three years, so we knew each other pretty well. She asked me how it was going every time I went in there. I always said good. We would chit-chat about local things happening, just small talk. She cashed the check for me. I said goodbye, walked out the door and got in my car.

I had to run by the grocery store to get a few groceries and by the time I got home it was around four in the afternoon. I quickly put my groceries away and jumped in the shower, got out and laid down on the couch. I wanted to see if I could get a nap in before I had to go out that evening.

I woke up to a loud, frantic knock on the door. It was Ellis. I sat up on the couch and groggily looked at my watch. It was already almost eight so I knew we were running late. I opened the door.

"What happened?" he asked.

"Man, I dozed off, let me grab a shirt and we'll head that way." I threw on a shirt and we headed off in the car.

I had the cash in my pocket. I was nervous, very nervous. I'd buy things here and there to turn them to make a few dollars, but nothing like this. Not guns, plural. Maybe *a* gun, but definitely not four assault rifles. Nowadays, if you get caught with an assault rifle you can do a lot of jail time, even if it's your first offense. The whole way there I had Ellis assure me these guys were good and there weren't going to be any issues. Of course, he did, but when he told me I could tell that he wasn't exactly sure, which made me even more nervous. There was a little bit of chill in the air. We had the windows down, we were driving on an oil road. It was about a fifteen-minute drive from town. Ellis always had any kind of meets out there, always by the oil derricks. There was a big tank there that held oil with ladders. In high school we would always climb to the top of them, drink beer or get high and just hang out for the night. The cops never came out that way.

As we pulled up, I noticed we were the first to arrive. I was a little relieved. I would prefer to be here waiting on them rather than them waiting on me. I pulled up by the tanks, killed the lights and got out. I was on the other side of the road and couldn't be seen by anyone if they drove by, not that anyone would be driving out here at this time of night. There were no houses around for miles.

As I got out I lit up a cigarette, and even in the middle of everything going on and being nervous and not knowing how things were going to work out, I still found myself thinking about Anna and why she was acting the way she did earlier that morning. There had to be something wrong. I couldn't get it out of my head. It was all I could think about, but I didn't get to think about it long enough because at that time two headlights came shining in.

They pulled up right in front of us in a black Chrysler 300. Three men stepped out, and they were not exactly who I expected to see getting out of a Chrysler 300. The driver had a black leather jacket on, which seemed about right, but the other two had camo shirts and hats. As sad as it was, I instantly felt a little better about the situation because they looked like good ol' boys. I threw my cigarette out and didn't move, just waited by the car for one of them to approach. As they got closer, I reached out and shook their hands.

"How's it going?" the guy in the leather jacket asked.

"Not bad, how are ya'll doing?" I said.

"Oh, we can't complain."

I never gave my name and he never gave his. I don't think either of us wanted to.

"So, I guess you're in the market for some guns?"

I glanced over at Ellis, and he gave me a nod. "Yeah, what ya got?" I said.

He nodded his head to follow me back to the trunk of the car. Having seen way too many movies, one thing I thought of was him grabbing me and throwing me in the trunk. Of course, my imagination was getting carried away. There was no reason for that to happen, but that was the first thing I always thought of.

We walked to the back of the car and he opened the trunk, inside was a crate. He pried the crate open. It contained a lot of gun parts. It looked like enough for some AK-47s, but there was no telling. I kind of looked at him funny and said, "Well, where are they?"

"Right there."

"No...there are pieces of guns in there, but where are the guns?"

"Well, we're not going to put them together for you. I mean, that was part of the deal. That's what we told Ellis. That's why you got such a good deal."

I shrugged my shoulders and sighed. I knew Ellis knew about this, he just didn't tell me. I peeked over the hood and looked at Ellis, knowing that Ellis had heard that, and he still wasn't looking at me because he knew I was pissed. I didn't have the slightest clue how to put these guns together. "Is everything here, at least?"

"Yeah, you've got everything here for four fully-automatic AK-47s."

My heart sank when he said those words. Fully automatic, that was illegal in every state. Get caught with fully automatic weapons and you are going to the federal penitentiary. And we were going to do this for a measly five-hundred-dollar profit? I was pissed. I was scared. I was nervous. I looked at him and he looked at me, and he could tell I wasn't very happy.

"Now listen, this is the deal we had. It's two grand for these four guns."

I looked over at Ellis and said, "Ellis, you didn't tell me they were fully automatic."

"Yeah, yeah they are."

I wasn't going to make a scene with Ellis, not in front of these guys. There was no telling what they were capable of or what they might do. Part of me wanted to shut the trunk and tell them to just keep going, sorry for the misunderstanding. But I knew how guys like this operated and after how far they had to drive, they were not going to tolerate that. They would probably beat the shit out of us, take our money and the guns.

Instead, I said, "That's fine." I reached in my pocket, handed them the two grand. He counted it. I grabbed the crate of guns and loaded them in the trunk of my car.

I shook his hand and told him it was nice to meet him. As they left I sat in the car with Ellis next to me and I was fuming. I looked over at him and said, "When were you going to tell me that these guns weren't put together? And that they are fully automatic?"

"Fully automatic, yeah, that's why they're worth so much. That's why we can make more money off them."

"So we're going to make five hundred on this deal, and risk spending twenty years in jail if we get caught?"

"Come on man," he said. "We aren't going to get caught."

"Bullshit! You don't know that. And how the hell do we put these things together?"

"I can do it, man. My brother was in the army, he showed me how. Plus, we can look on the internet if we have to. We can put them together, that's not a problem."

I started the car up and pulled out onto the oil road. "Here's the deal: we're going to dump them off at the shop, in the back, where nobody can see them. Then your ass is getting up in the morning, I don't care how early you have to get up, and you're going to put these together. Then you're going to call your contact and set up a time tomorrow or the next day to get rid of these."

"Yeah, yeah man, I'll do that. I've already talked to him and Eddie said he can pick them up tomorrow or the next day."

"Eddie? Eddie who?" I asked.

"Eddie Stevens."

As soon as he said that name I immediately got angry.

"Eddie Stevens? You're selling guns to Eddie Stevens?" Eddie Stevens was the local screw-up. He had been to jail several times. He ran around with three or four guys and between them all they had about a one hundred IQ. They graduated about four years ahead of me, they weren't bright, and everybody knew when they did something stupid. "If Eddie Stevens gets caught with these guns, fully automatic rifles, where do you think he is going to tell them he got them?"

"Man, he's not keeping them. He's getting rid of them. He's already got somebody else, his uncle in Colorado wants them. He is going to take them up there."

"Oh my God, this is the worst thing we have ever had to do. I don't feel comfortable selling to him."

"Well, he's the only person I know who wants them. I don't know, trust me man, he will get rid of 'em and nobody will know anything."

"How the hell did it get to this point?"

"What do you mean?" he asked.

"Why the hell am I driving around at nine o'clock at night with a bunch of illegal guns in my trunk, just so I can get by? This is so no worth it."

I was frustrated and taking my anger out on Ellis, even though it was mostly his fault we got into this mess. But still, he did it for me. He wasn't going to make hardly anything on these guns. He was taking on just as much risk as I was and he was doing it for me, that's why he was such a great friend, but I was still frustrated.

"Well, I guess that's what we'll do then. You can put them together, we'll get rid of them to Eddie, clean our prints off and if anybody asks, we didn't have anything to do with it. You just make sure he comes alone and he doesn't have four or five people with him seeing that he bought them from us."

"I will. I'll take care of it."

I could tell Ellis felt bad. He knew he had screwed me in a way.

At that time I noticed a car pull out from a back road right behind us, speed up and get on our ass.

"Do you know that car?"

Ellis started to turn around but I told him to just look in the mirror.

"No, that looks like a cop car."

"Looks like it could be Dwayne," I said. "He's on duty tonight, saw him earlier. Holy shit."

"Just be cool, drive the speed limit. We'll be fine."

44

"No, we won't be fine. He hates me."

"What do you mean?" Ellis asked.

"He's never liked me. I dated his ex-girlfriend right out of high school and he's been pissed at me ever since. It has been years and he still carries a grudge. He's pulled me over a dozen times just to give me shit."

"He doesn't know anything. He can't look in our trunk."

"He can if he gets a search warrant."

"He's got to have probable cause."

"In a small town like this, you really think so?"

About that time, he lit up his lights.

"Oh, shit!" I looked over at Ellis. He was on his phone, calling someone. "What are you doing?" I asked him.

"Trust me."

I drove about another quarter-mile and slowly pulled over, just as Ellis was getting off the phone. I put my hands on the steering wheel, I knew the drill. The cop came walking up to the car with his light shining in my face. Sure enough, it was Dwayne.

"Mr. Hagen, you were speeding back there weren't ya?"

"No, sir, no I wasn't." Normally, I would be an asshole to him. But tonight I had ten-to-twenty years sitting in the trunk of my car. I was going to be a little more warm and polite this evening.

"Why don't you step on out of the car," he told me.

"Is there a problem, Dwayne? I wasn't speeding."

"Just step out of the car." I did as he said then he added "You too," shining his light over at Ellis. So he got out of the car, too. "Put your hands on the hood."

We put our hands on the hood. I looked over at Ellis, shaking my head. I knew this was it. All the stupid things I'd done, they were all coming to this, to this very point in my life. This would be what I would be remembered for, the guy who had four fully-automatic assault rifles in the trunk of his car. And in a small town like this I would be viewed as a terrorist.

The cop shined his light in my car. "How much have ya'll had to drink tonight?"

Thankfully, I hadn't even had time for a drink because we had been running so late.

"None, Dwayne. We haven't been drinking at all tonight."

"Smells like alcohol."

We both knew the car didn't smell like alcohol. He was busting my chops.

"No, Dwayne, there's no alcohol in the vehicle, and we have not been drinking."

"Well, what you got in the trunk?"

Immediately, I knew I was screwed. Dwayne wasn't the kind of cop to get a search warrant. Even if I told him no, he would still open the trunk. And even if he found the rifles illegally, I would still get in trouble. They would say I was acting aggressively or something along those lines to give them an excuse to open my trunk.

He reached in, grabbed the keys and walked over to open the trunk. and about that time his radio started going off. He walked off about twenty feet in the distance. He was on the radio for about ten seconds. He ran back and threw the keys to me and ran to his car and peeled off. I held the keys in my hand. I looked at Ellis and he had a big grin on his face. I looked up at the sky and said *Thank you, God*. I had gotten away with this one. I looked back at Ellis and asked why he was grinning.

"I called Lisa. Told her to report hearing gunfire down the road from our house and to start screaming."

I smiled. "So that's where he went."

"Yeah, but once he's there he'll realize there's nothing going on, so we have got to get these out of here."

"Ellis, you are a genius. You are off the hook."

We immediately jumped back in the car and headed to the shop to unload the guns.

CHAPTER 6

The next morning, after lying in bed for an hour, I finally got up and thought I'd be early to work for once. I knew Ellis would be there because I told him to go in early to put the guns together. Maybe I was a little too hard on him last night, I thought, so I figured I'd go in and help him. But like always, something seemed to go wrong. After I'd gotten out of the shower and actually ate something for breakfast, my car wouldn't start. This was the third time in the last month I had issues with it, but luckily I knew exactly what it was. I jumped out of the car, popped the hood, shook the battery cables and got back in. It started fine.

I got to work a little before eight. When I arrived, Ellis was there, and he had all the guns put together, all but the last one and he was about to finish that one up. We didn't talk much. There wasn't a whole lot to say. I could tell by the look in his eyes that it was stressful on him, too. It was easy for me to forget that he was right there by my side. He would have had to take just as much responsibility as I'd have if we would have got caught. I can only image what he had to deal with when he went home last night.

"So, how'd it go when you got home?" I asked him.

He paused for a second, looked up and just shook his head.

"That good, huh? Just look at it this way, you get those put together, we'll make another shady deal with a couple of assholes from town, and make a couple hundred bucks apiece."

He paused again and looked up at me. I could tell he didn't appreciate my sarcasm. I walked into my office and sat down. I started to go through the books. I tried to decide how much money we'd made and how much money we'd lost. This was one of my least favorite tasks to do at work because no matter what the numbers never added up to what I felt they should. We weren't making enough money, but that's how it normally was. It seemed like I worked harder and made less money than I ever have. I was making more and more less-than-legal deals lately.

I'd planned on leaving early. I was going to stop by my folks' house and have dinner like I always did on my father's birthday. The only good thing about mine and my father's relationship was that he didn't expect gifts or even a card. It was pointless to do anything for him. He didn't appreciate it. He could obviously care less. As he grew older, I could tell life was slowly meaning less and less to him.

I finally left the shop around two in the afternoon. Since I didn't sleep much the night before I was hoping I could go home, possibly get a little nap. As I walked in the door and threw my keys on the table, I laid down on the couch. I started to doze off and my phone went off. It was a text message from Lady.

I hadn't spoken to her in a day or so, so she was just checking in to see how I was doing and wanted to know the next time we could see each other. Of course, I didn't want to tell her the truth. I was broke and I couldn't afford to see her. Spending time with Lady always seemed to be expensive, and I didn't want her to see me as I really was...as the twenty-something-year-old broken down worthless person that I am. She always seemed to hold me on a pedestal, and I just didn't want to break her heart and let her know who I really was. I didn't want to tell her that I was a failure, my business was going under. You would think the opinion of a stripper wouldn't matter to me. Strangely, she was one of the more positive relationships in my life. I texted her back and told her everything was good and maybe this weekend. Of course, I knew that was a lie as soon as I sent the message to her, but it would buy me some time to come up with some other excuse that I couldn't see her. I never could tell how she truly felt about me. That was the thing with girls like Lady, never could tell if they cared about you or not, and I don't think I'd ever know.

I started to doze again, and my phone rang. I looked at it and it was Anna. I pushed the ignore button and let it go to voicemail. It wasn't anything personal towards her. I was tired, in a bad mood, and that was just one more conversation I didn't want to have.

I woke up a couple of hours later to my phone ringing. It was my mother. She had called just to make sure I was coming. I told her I was about to head out the door and I'd be there in a little bit. It had gotten cool outside, so I grabbed my jacket as I headed out the door.

On the drive out to my folks' house, I couldn't help but feel guilty for dreading this night so much. I always wished things were different with my father, but they just weren't going to be, and the drive didn't help either. It was just the right amount of time for me to think about the things that I regretted about my father and our relationship, but as I'd gotten older I decided that I didn't want to argue with him and just tolerate him. I figure you can't change who your parents are, you can only decide how you want to deal with them.

I pulled up in the driveway and, of course, I was the only one there. My folks were hermits, not literally, but they didn't go out much — to church, maybe to the grocery store a couple of times a month and that was about it. So, having friends wasn't real high on their to-do list. I walked in the front door and my mom was in the kitchen getting everything ready. She gave me a big hug.

"How are you doing?" she asked me.

"Good, doing great, how are ya'll?"

"Oh, we're good. I'm glad you could make it."

My mom always tried to hide the fact that my father and I had a bad relationship, but she knew. She avoided talking about it, pretended like everything was great. Of course, their relationship wasn't that great either, but she had learned to deal with him and it was too late in her life to make changes...like getting a divorce or standing up for herself. So, she just made the best of a bad situation. My dad was sitting in his chair when I walked in.

"Hey, Pop."

"Hey," he said.

"Well, happy birthday."

"Thank you."

"How have you been feeling lately?"

"Oh, you know, same-o, same-o."

I sat down on the couch across from him and tried to spend a little bit of time with him.

"So, how's the business doing?" he asked.

"Oh, you know, same-o, same-o."

I couldn't tell him the truth. I didn't want to tell him the business was going under, slowly but surely. That would just give him a little more satisfaction, but maybe I should have told him. That would be the best birthday present he had ever gotten...hearing about his son's failures, he would love that.

We spent the next twenty minutes in small talk, nothing big, of course he threw in a few remarks here and there about my love life, asking when I was going to get married and this and that. I just played along, acted like I was happy being single and being married wasn't what I cared for.

We sat down for dinner and my mom put on a show like she was happy as could be. After we finished dinner, my mom was serving cake and then she asked me how Anna was doing, which had always been a touchy subject with my father. I think at some point I told him how I felt about her, trying to have a father-son moment with him, hoping for a little bit of encouragement or some advice, but that's not what I got from him. What I got from him was a long lecture about how she was married and how I wasn't good enough for her.

"She's doing pretty good, I guess," I said.

My mother started to speak, "Well, I'd spoken to her the other day —"

My father quickly interrupted. "You need to stay away from her."

I dropped the fork on the plate, and looked at him with a confused look. He stared back at me.

"Why is that?" I asked.

"She's married."

"Well I know that, Dad, we're not dating, we're just friends."

"Well maybe that would have been different if you hadn't screwed things up."

I knew then what he was doing. I'd worn out my welcome, and it was time for me to leave, which is probably what I should have done. It was never what he said but how he said it and the expressions on his face when he said it. My mother looked at me and she didn't even have to say anything. I knew it was time for me to go.

"Exactly how did I screw things up, Dad?"

"I don't know, how about your drinking and all of your nonsense."

"My nonsense?"

"Yeah, that's why you're working out of an old run-down gas station, can't even hold a job because you can't handle authority."

"Well, Dad, to be honest with you, I'm surprised it took you this long. I was here almost an hour before you said anything negative."

"I'm just telling you how it is, Tyler. You do stupid stuff and you get nowhere in life."

"Dad, I just came over here to wish you happy birthday and have a nice dinner. Why do you constantly feel the need to remind me that in your eyes I'm nothing?"

"That's not what I'm doing, son."

"No, Dad, it is what you're doing. It's what you've always done. You find any possible opportunity to let me in on that fact."

"I'm just saying, if you wouldn't make stupid decisions—"

I stopped him in the middle of his sentence. "I don't want to hear it."

I stood up and slid my chair back quickly and angrily. My mother got up and said, "No, Tyler." I was about to speak when there was a knock on the door. I looked at mom and dad, not knowing who it could possibly be. My mom answered the door and in walked Anna.

"Hey! There's the birthday boy!" Anna said.

Of course Anna didn't know we were about to finish up a screaming match. My mom gave her a big hug and they started laughing and it was like the argument never happened. I grabbed my plate, set it on the counter and walked out the door and passed Anna without saying a word to her. Before I could open my car door Anna had run outside.

"What are you doing?" she asked.

"Oh, I think it's about time for me to leave."

"Well I just got here. What's wrong?"

She could tell I was frustrated and angry, I was rubbing my forehead.

"You know Anna, after about an hour of listening to him, I am just about ready to go."

She didn't have to ask what the argument was about I'd confided in her for years about my father, and of course with her being good friends with my mother I could only imagine what they talked about.

"Tyler, you have to get over whatever it is between you and your father."

I sighed and leaned back against the car. "Get over what?"

"Your father loves you."

"I never said he didn't, Anna. I have no doubt in my mind that he loves me. I have no doubt in my mind that he loves my mother, but I have seen the ways he treats her. Maybe not so much now, but growing up, he was a real asshole."

"You're both adults, you need to talk about this."

"We have. We talked about it every time I come over here. It's gotten worse since the accident. I wasn't even driving and he blames me."

"No he doesn't, Tyler."

"Yes he does. It's been even worse since the accident. He felt like I should have done something. Maybe he is right. Maybe I should have done something."

She looked at me almost as if she was going to cry. Anna was never the type of person to give up hope but I could tell she was going to give up on this conversation. She walked toward me and gave me a big hug.

She stepped back and said, "You have to find a way to deal with this. Maybe not talking to him, but talking to somebody. You let him control your life and he's not the type of person who should have any control over how you feel or what you do. You've spent your whole life trying to get his approval when no matter what you do, he just might not be the type of man who will ever give it."

With her hands on my shoulders and my hands at her waist, I leaned my head down and for a minute I didn't think about the fact that I was in love with her or anything. I just took comfort in the fact that she was right there with me. She stepped back, realizing we were too close. It would have gotten awkward.

"Thanks, Anna, you've…always been there for me." For a second I'd forgotten all about the argument so I asked her "When we had coffee the other day, I felt like you wanted to tell me something but you didn't, you were holding back. You always told me that I could come to you for anything, now tell me what you have on your mind."

She smiled half-heartedly, trying to force it out.

"It was nothing. Don't worry about it. I'm going in to visit with your mother and wish your father happy birthday. I'll call you later."

I watched her walk away and when she got to the front door she took one last glance at me. I got in the car and started it and left as quickly as I could. I was trying to put as much distance between my father and me as I could.

CHAPTER 7

As I was putting my parents' house further and further in my rearview, I still couldn't help but get angry, thinking about what my father had said to me and the fact that he always seemed to find a way to get under my skin, and it was getting harder and harder the older I got to shrug it off. I didn't want to make a big scene in front of my mother or Anna, but I couldn't help but feel like less of a man for not really telling him how I felt. I have always wondered how we haven't gotten into a physical altercation over the years. I don't know if it was because I was a coward or just because I was a better person than he was.

I reached in the glovebox and grabbed a few Vicodin and chased them down with a warm beer I had in the backseat. I knew in a few minutes that would help me feel better about the whole situation. My mind was a little bit at ease thinking about Anna, and the fact that it felt like things were pretty good between us, but then my mind would wander and I'd start to think about how things could have been and I'd get frustrated all over again. No matter what I did, it seemed like it was never enough. I also felt like even if I was with her I'd never feel like I was good enough. And of course, Anna knew about my drug problem. At least, I assumed she did. In a town this small people talk. I am sure she would know. Even if things were different, I don't think things would be that much different between us. I always did find myself questioning her loyalty to me, even though that didn't make sense. She was always such a better friend to me than I was to her. I didn't see the benefit for her. I always felt at some point in the back of my mind that she did have some sort of feelings for me. I never really had the opportunity to explore that. Of course, as soon as those thoughts would come up, thoughts of every bad decision and mistake I made in the past would also come up, forcing me to believe, of course, there was no way she cared about me.

I rolled the windows down in the car and turned the radio up as loud as it would go, anything to drown out my thoughts. I fumbled around in the backseat until I found an almost-empty bottle of vodka. I took a few pulls off of it, hoping it would calm me down, and it soon did. I got my cell phone out and decided it was too early to go home, so I decided to call Ellis and asked him to meet me in town for a few beers. He agreed, of course. He was always there when I needed him. I could hear his girlfriend yapping in the background. I am sure it was something negative about me, but I've known Ellis so long that in a weird way he would always put me before her. The fact that I was kind of his employer helped, too.

As I drove into town, I pulled up to Sam's, the local drinking tavern. It was the only place to get a drink in town. It was very run down and the drinks weren't even that good, and most of the people that came to this place were looking just to get drunk. It wasn't exactly the place for a whole lot of excitement. There was usually about the same few cars every time you drove by the place...locals spending their entire paycheck just to get drunk. That's how it was for some people, and I can definitely understand. You work all week long, then spend your paycheck to forget it. Didn't make a whole lot of sense, but what else was there to do?

As I pulled into the bar, I could see that Ellis was already there. I'm sure he was already in town and that is why he beat me. I walked through the door and I could instantly smell cigarette smoke and stale beer. The joint was really small. It probably could only hold about thirty people. Of course, there was usually only about ten people in it. The place used to be a pool hall and Sam had bought it about twenty years ago and turned it into a bar. The place was just a metal building. You could see the chicken wire over the insulation, and the beams were still around the wall. He never painted it or did anything to it. You could see the air-conditioning ducts just hanging there. Sam didn't exactly spend much money on renovating on this place. Just enough for a few tables, a few bar stools, and a lot of whiskey.

I knew in a couple of hours the smell wouldn't bother me much because I'd be very drunk. I walked into the bar and sat down next to Ellis and he gave me a pat on the back and said, "How's things?"

I shrugged, ordered a drink then quickly ordered a second one. Ellis was a good man to have around when you had problems. He was good to have around because you would never find yourself talking about something that you didn't want to talk about. He wouldn't ask what was bothering you or try to get specifics. He would just let you talk, let you say what you wanted to say. Half the time we could spend all evening talking and it wouldn't even be about what was on my mind, but by the end of the night I'd feel so much better.

As we sat there talking and drinking, the door of the bar opened up and a familiar face walked in. It was Jerry. The younger brother of Eddie Stevens, the man I was supposed to sell guns to. I had not seen him in a while. He was my main source to where I could get my drugs. He really didn't deal with a whole lot of Vicodin, so I hadn't seem him lately, but he always had heroin, crack cocaine, oxy, whatever you needed. We didn't really know each other that well. We just knew each other through drugs. Half the time I was around him I was so high I couldn't remember anything we talked about.

Jerry came up and sat a couple of seats down, lit up a cigarette and asked me how I was doing and nodded. After his first drink, he nodded with his head for me to follow him outside. I knew what it was, but the kind of night I was having I was down. We walked outside and over to his truck and he asked me if I needed anything. I asked him what he had. Of course, he had a little bit of everything. I was a little short on cash, so I bought a couple of oxy from him and chewed them up quickly, gave him the money and went back in. He didn't follow me. He got in his truck and left. He must have been making a stop to see if there was anybody there he could get rid of anything to, and I just so happened to be his lucky customer.

As I sat at the bar, I could feel everybody's eyes staring at me. They knew him and they knew me and they knew what just went down in the parking lot, but I couldn't care less, at least not in front of these people. Ellis would never say anything to me about it. He had been through this before. He had his issues when he was younger. He had gotten pretty straight over the past year, so he was the last person to judge me. He wouldn't even bring it up.

I had a couple more shots of whiskey and another beer waiting for the oxy to kick in, and as soon as they did, I felt better. I didn't even think about the conversation I had with my dad. I wasn't angry anymore. I was happy and felt great. Ellis and I sat and talked for about another hour until I was good and drunk and high.

We walked out to our cars, said our goodbyes, and he left. I sat in my car and looked at my clock. It was almost midnight. Knowing I had to go to work the next day, I still didn't want to go home, but I wasn't in my right mind either. I started my car up and pulled out to the end of the bar's driveway. I was about to turn right to head home but for some reason I turned left. Guess I wasn't ready to call it a night. So, as I was driving through the empty streets of Juniper with the radio on and the windows down, I was feeling great.

I don't know how it happened, but I ended up turning down the road that Anna lived on. I don't know if it was by chance or maybe it was my subconscious leading me that way. I had no intentions of stopping, but I felt like once I got to her driveway I should. I knew I'd live to regret the decision I was about to make, but I had to see her. I couldn't quit thinking about the last few weeks, how every conversation felt like it was open-ended and that there was more to be said. I don't know why I felt like I was entitled to drive up to her house at that hour, but at that very moment I didn't feel like I was doing anything wrong. I knew I was drunk, so I tried to carefully pull into the driveway but still hit the curb and ran over a couple of her trashcans, making a loud noise. She lived in a very nice wooden two-story old plantation-style house with a screened-in porch.

I pulled up in the driveway and killed the engine. Before I could even open my door the porch light was on, and Anna was at the door. I opened up my door and started to step out. I could hear Anna talking to someone inside the house. I didn't pay any attention. She opened the screen door and shut the door behind her and came out in a nightgown. I could tell she had just woken up and I started to feel guilty, and then when she came outside in her night clothes, I started to slowly realize the mistake I had made.

"Tyler, is that you?" she asked.

"Hey, Anna, I was just in the neighborhood and—"

"What are you doing? It's after midnight. You can't do this."

"Listen, Anna, I just needed to talk to you."

"Well, can't it wait until morning?"

"Well...no it can't."

Immediately, I realized the situation I had just put myself and her in. Even though I was far from sober, I started to realize the consequences of the decision I'd made. I didn't know what to do. I didn't know if I should just cover myself or just go for it.

"Is this about your dad?"

"No, this is about you and me."

She sighed. "Tyler, there is no 'you and me.'"

"The last few times we talked there was something you needed to tell me but you wouldn't."

"No, Tyler, there is nothing I need to say."

"I don't believe you."

"This is not the time or the place for us to be having this conversation. You need to go home and we'll meet in the morning and talk about this."

"Why can't we talk about it now?"

"Tyler, it's after midnight. You came up here and you woke me up."

I immediately started to feel bad and started to apologize. She stopped me and said, "Don't worry about it, it's not a big deal."

Once she said that I started to think about all the things that I'd said or done inappropriately and I always felt like I had an excuse. That I was high or I was drunk, but she seemed to always let it go. She seemed to always roll with the punches. In the next quick seconds I began to think about that, and I couldn't understand why my behavior was okay with her, why it seemed like no matter what I did, she was always there for me. There were very few people in the world who would allow this, and even fewer reasons as to why they would allow it. Either they feel sorry for you or they were in love with you. I knew she didn't feel sorry for me because growing up she had it worse than I did. So, I started to think between me being intoxicated and everything that had happened, I began to think that possibly she could have feelings.

"Why do you let me get away with this?" I could tell she was getting impatient.

She crossed her arms. "What do you mean?"

"I show up at your house at midnight, run over your trash cans, constantly screwing shit up, there's no reason for you to put up with this. Unless—"

She quickly stopped me because I think she knew what I was going to say.

"You need to go home," she said.

Then about that time I heard the screen door open and it was Kevin, her husband. He had come out in his pajamas and a T-shirt holding a baseball bat in his hand.

"Honey, what is going on?" He started to walk down the steps.

Anna quickly turned and told him, "Kevin, it's okay, go inside."

"No, it's not okay. It's midnight. What's he doing here?"

"Kevin, please, it's okay. Go inside."

"What the hell is he thinking? Coming up here this time of night."

About that time I interrupted. I probably shouldn't have, but I didn't like his tone of voice. It was too late for me. I already made the decision and had to stick with it.

"Why don't you listen to her and go inside?" I said.

He came down the stairs and walked about halfway with the bat pointed at me.

"I tell you what, how 'bout me and you take it to the end of the driveway and we can solve this right now."

As he started to walk towards me, Anna got between us and started pushing him back towards the house. She whispered something to him in his ear as she pushed him towards the house. I couldn't hear what she was saying, and I was starting to get insecure about what she must had been saying. I quickly said, "That's fine, I can go right now."

Anna turned around. "Dammit, Tyler, get in your car."

I stood there and paused for a few seconds. I didn't want her to think she had that much control over me. As I stared at her husband, I slowly walked over to my car and opened the door. I shut the door he was walking inside, and I could see Anna put her head down and shake it like she was frustrated and didn't know what to do. I reached in my backseat and saw the bottle of vodka. It had about a swig left in it. I quickly drank it and tossed the bottle in the back. As Anna walked towards me I could hear her flip-flops scraping the gravel on the driveway. She was walking very slow as if she was trying to think of what she needed to say before she got there. She put her hands on my car door and leaned in and she started to say, "Tyler—"

But I interrupted her and said, "Anna, you didn't answer my question. Why do you put up with this? Why are you always there when I need you?"

She looked as me, her eyes glassy, almost as if she was going to cry. Then I saw a facial expression I had never seen on her before. She was so vulnerable at that very moment. She knew she had to choose her next words carefully because they could dramatically change her life. She hung her head down for a second. She pulled it up and I saw one single teardrop roll down her cheek. "Tyler, we..." but then about that time the screen door opened and Caroline, her four-year-old daughter, came running outside in her pajamas. She ran up to Anna and Anna turned around and picked her up.

"Mommy, what's going on?"

"Nothing, sweetie."

"Hey, Caroline. Did I wake you up?"

"No, I was supposed to be asleep, but I wasn't really asleep."

Anna grinned and laughed, then looked over at me. "I will see you tomorrow."

I started my car up knowing I wasn't going to get the answer I needed or wanted now. As I was backing out of the driveway Anna was walking inside. She turned around and gave me another look, and I noticed all the lights were now on in her house. I was sure her husband was waiting on her to come back in. I started to feel guilty. I had just crossed the line that for the last fifteen years I promised myself I wouldn't cross. I put her in a situation I swore I'd never do.

The guilt was hard to deal with. The drive home was long. There was no radio this time. It was just me alone with my thoughts. I knew I wouldn't be able to sleep, but I had to try.

Chapter 8

I lay in bed, staring at the clock on the wall. Hours had passed, and I still hadn't slept at all. I kept reliving the conversation and the events that had happened last night, trying to find answers, trying to find a way out of the mess I had put myself in. I knew there wasn't one. Over and over I kept replaying it in my head. I was trying to justify the decisions I'd made, trying to find comfort in what had happened. I'd set myself up for failure once again. I had put myself in a situation where I couldn't win.

A sickening pain was rising in my stomach. I couldn't push it down. It reminded me of the day I detoxed. The hallucinations, and that horrible sickening feeling I had, but that day I had a voice comforting me, or at least I thought I did. I didn't have that now. I just laid there, dreading every minute that passed because I had to get up. I had to prepare myself for what was ahead. I didn't know how Anna would react. I didn't know if I would ever see her again after what I did. There was no way I could come back from this. I stared at the clock and watched it tick, until finally seven-o'clock hit and I decided to get up.

I put the coffee on, I took a handful of pain killers hoping that I could maybe just go through the day without any possible consequences. What was I thinking? Driving over there in the middle of the night, acting that way. I had so much to say to her, but I could never say it. I don't know if I was more afraid of her telling me to get lost or telling me that she felt the same way. It was a losing situation either way. I wasn't good enough for her. I was living in a world without answers. I could only lose every day. Every decision I made was the wrong one, and if I would have made the opposite decision, I would have had to live without saying what I wanted to say and I couldn't do that either.

I sat on the couch drinking coffee. I was scrolling through my phone looking for someone to call, maybe someone had answers. At a time like this when I was younger, I could always talk to my brother before he passed. He was always open-minded. I could talk to him about anything. It was days like this that really made me think about him. It was just more of regret. It seemed like every day was getting worse. The decisions I made and the consequences that followed. After I finished my coffee I got up and took a cold shower, hoping it would wake me up. It was almost painful, but in a way I felt like I was punishing myself for what I had done.

As I got out of the shower, I could hear my phone ringing. The first thing that popped in my head was that it was Anna calling. Basically, my stomach sank and I started feeling nauseous. I walked over and looked. It wasn't Anna, it was mother. I just hit the decline button. It wasn't a good time to talk, not to anybody. I got dressed, made another cup of coffee to take with me, and got in my car and left. Sitting in my car driving down the road, all it did was remind me of the night before. I felt mentally and physically horrible, and the smell of the beer and the alcohol in my car made it worse. I took the long way. I had left early enough. I was going to get to work earlier than I had been in months.

As I pulled up to the shop, Ellis was already there, which was not a surprise. I parked the car and got out. Ellis was at the other end of the shop. I just gave him a wave and headed into my office. I could tell by the way he was looking at me he was confused. Me getting there that early just wasn't normal.

I went into my office and sat down, and leaned back in my chair and rubbed my head. I knew this was going to be a long day. I was exhausted from not getting any sleep, but at the same time I could shut my eyes and nothing would happen. My brain was filled with so many random thoughts. I was ashamed and I felt guilty for what I had done. Anna deserved so much better. I was a grown child, the way I acted, waking up her daughter in the middle of the night, her husband having to come outside, and the bad thing about it was he did not even deserve that. He was a decent guy. He did well for her. He treated her well. I tried so hard to hate him, but I just couldn't. He was very tolerant of Anna and me and our friendship. I think he was that way because he did not have a choice. He knew he won the lottery being with her. I think he knew that she was so much better than him, so he never gave her too much trouble for being friends with me. Of course, I never felt like he knew the extent of our friendship. I never felt like he knew how often we talked or saw each other. He worked out of town a lot. I don't think Anna would deliberately lie to him, but I don't feel like she ever told him the truth, either.

I sat at my desk, flipping through paperwork I hadn't looked at in about a week. There were several payments that were past due. This was the day I normally made phone calls trying to collect money, but I just didn't feel like doing it today. I glanced over at the clock and it read eight-thirty. I sighed out loud. I had only been there an hour, but it felt much longer. About that time Ellis walked in.

"Hey man, what are you doing up here so early?"

"Couldn't sleep," I said. "Thought I would come in and take care of a few things."

"Is everything all right?"

I didn't even look up when he asked. I didn't feel like talking about it, not yet. Enough time hadn't passed that I felt like I had analyzed this enough to talk about it. He was my best friend. He was the one person I should talk to, but I still found it hard to find the words to what had happened. I still felt ashamed and embarrassed.

"Yeah," I said, "same-o, same-o."

"Alright. What's the plan for today?"

"Well, I was going to ask you. You seem to know more about what is going on than I do."

He kind of laughed under his breath. I looked at him and grinned. "What about the other thing, where we at on that?"

"You mean the guns?" he asked.

So much for subtlety. "Yeah. The guns."

"I talked to him. It's setup for tonight. I'll call him and make sure, but everything is set."

"Good. Good deal. Where are we going to meet him at?"

"The storage buildings on the other side of town. I didn't figure you wanted to meet him here."

"No, not at all."

I always tried to keep those types of business deals away from my legitimate business in town. I never wanted people to get the idea of what I did or what I had to do. Being such a small town, if I wasn't careful everybody would know my business and everybody would know what I did. I think people had somewhat of an idea, but not enough of an idea for it to be common knowledge.

Ellis stood in the doorway. I think he was waiting for me to say something else. Ellis wasn't an idiot. He knew I had things going on that were bothering me. The anniversary of my brother's death was coming up, and he knew how I felt about Anna, and he knew that was a struggle I dealt with every day. He would always listen, but he never gave a whole lot of advice, which I appreciated because I always felt like if you didn't know what to say, then you shouldn't say anything at all, and that is what he did. He would say a few words, but the ones he did use he chose carefully and usually they had meaning.

"Alright, I'm going to make some phone calls and see if I can get some of this money collected and maybe get us a paycheck this week."

"I'm going to put a lacquer finish on that set of tables and chairs back there," he said. "Start making a few things we can put in the arts and crafts festival since we don't have any definite orders lined up yet."

"Okay man, that's cool. Maybe we'll have something by the end of the week."

He nodded and went back to the shop.

I sifted through paperwork for about an hour and half, making several phone calls, getting nowhere. People always paid, they just took their time. I think people mistook my kindness for weakness and they would take advantage. I have had to knock on a few doors, but nothing ever got crazy.

After I was done making phone calls, I cleaned off my desk and put everything up and made a few notes for next week, things I needed to do. When my shop used to be a gas station, it had a bell for people who pulled up and it would ding. About that time, I heard it go off so I peeked through the blinds. I would like to say I was surprised, but I wasn't. It was Anna pulling up.

My heart starting beating faster, and I stepped back away from the blinds with an anxious feeling. Part of me thought she would come by, but another part of me thought maybe she would just let time run its course and let things die down a little bit. To be honest, that was what I was hoping. It was too soon. I hadn't had any sleep. I still didn't know what to say to her. I didn't know how to explain myself. Part of me wanted to walk out the back door and just keep walking, avoid the whole thing. Mistakes were made and there was nothing I could say. I didn't want to tell her it was a mistake. I couldn't tell her it was a mistake. I didn't want her thinking I was just a weak, pathetic person.

I watched her walk up to Ellis. I couldn't hear what they were saying. They only talked for a few seconds, then he pointed to my office. She walked briskly towards my office as if she had a purpose. She had a very stern look on her face, not so much anger, but more a sense of purpose. I went and sat down in my chair behind my desk and pulled out some papers, trying to act busy. I didn't want her to see that I was just sitting in my chair twiddling my thumbs.

She knocked on the door, opened it up, then looked at me. Her facial expression changed. It went from stern, filled with purpose, to filled with vulnerability. She stood in the doorway for a few seconds. I kept my head down like I didn't know she was there. She didn't know what to say, I knew she didn't. She cleared her throat so that I would know she was there. I looked up and acted like I was surprised to see her and said hello.

"Tyler, we need to talk."

I shut the open notebook on my desk and leaned back in my chair. "Yeah, I kind of figured this was coming."

"Last night—"

I stopped her in the middle of her sentence. "I'm sorry. Listen, I had had a few drinks, I don't know what I was thinking."

"No, you do know what you were thinking," she said. "You can't come to my house in the middle of the night and wake my kid and my husband up."

The way she said *husband* was like she had said a thousand words using just that one word.

I sighed. I noticed I had put my head down, looking at the ground. "Look, Anna, I am sorry. I don't have words to explain what I did. Like I said, I had a few drinks—"

She cut me off.

"Tyler..."

I could see a confused, frustrated look on her face. She didn't know how to say what she wanted to say. Or she didn't know what she was going to say. Then, that stern look came across her face again.

"You know, it is just unacceptable. You can't come to my house in the middle of the night. I understand what you are feeling but—" and then I cut her off again.

"Listen, Anna, let's just leave it as a mistake."

I wanted to say so much more. I wanted to look into her eyes and tell her that she was the most beautiful person inside and out, that the only reason why there was a little bit of good in me was because she existed and was a part of my life, but I couldn't say those things because having her in my life just a little bit was worth more to me than risking losing it all.

I got up out of my chair and walked towards her, and as I got closer she took a half-step back. She was nervous, I could tell. I don't know if she was afraid of what I would say or if she was afraid of what she might say. I looked at her and I could tell that she felt something for me, but part of me could not imagine that she did. As I got close, she put her head down.

"I appreciate you being tolerant and patient with me, I really do," I said. "I can't say I am sorry enough."

There was few seconds of silence as she was staring at her shoes. Finally, she said, "You know, Tyler, if you would just go to church and try to—"

I turned away from her out of frustration because I didn't want to have this conversation again. Then I turned back around and said, "Anna, don't."

"You have to understand. God loves you. He has a plan."

"No, I can't live with myself thinking that there is someone up there that has allowed everything that has happened in my life to happen. If I could do anything to help anybody, to stop any kind of pain, I would, and you are telling me there is a God up there that just watches us billions of people go through pain every day? I can't put my faith in something like that. But I could put my faith in someone like you."

She looked up with a very surprised look on her face, and she reached out and grabbed the back of my elbow and pulled herself closer. She looked up at me and I realized why she had put her head down. She had let a tear roll down her face. This was the second time I had seen her cry in less than twenty-four hours. I was not happy with myself. It seemed like every time I was around her lately I would either get her in trouble with her husband or I would make her cry, and I wanted to be everything in her life except for that.

I didn't even realize it, but we were inches apart, and with her staring in my eyes I reached up with my right thumb and wiped the tear from her cheek. I slowly leaned in to give her a hug, and she laid her head against my chest, and my chin was on top of her head, and I could feel this sigh of relief in her body as if she had been waiting for that for so long. I, too, felt like I could breathe for the first time having her that close to me, feeling like we were breathing as one. It was only seconds, but it felt like an eternity.

For the first time, I felt like I could say what I wanted to say. All those thoughts and words and phrases began to run through my head. I felt like I had been cleansed and I could finally say what I wanted to say, I could tell her how I felt.

Before any of that could happen, though, she yanked herself back, realizing what she had done was the worst possible thing she could have done. She wiped her face quickly. She looked at me in the eyes for a couple seconds then put her head down.

"You can't come over to my house."

I took a step back and realized that I couldn't say anything. I was a coward. There was nothing for me to say to her at this point in time. She let herself go for a few seconds, and at that point, it was probably the greatest few seconds of my life. The stern look had come back on her face as if she had rehearsed the conversation a hundred times.

"I've got to go," she said. "I just wanted to stop by and clarify that."

I just said okay. I wanted to say more, but couldn't. She walked away and got in her car without even saying goodbye. I leaned in the doorway, wondering what I did to deserve this.

CHAPTER 9

I stood there, leaning against the wall, and watched her get into her car. As she drove off, I could feel my face starting to tingle, and I was doing everything I could to keep the tears from coming out. Everything was getting worse. Part of me was relieved that it was over. I knew that moment was going to come eventually. I was just glad it was behind me now. But the thoughts still consumed me—of her, my life, and the decisions I had been making lately.

I slowly walked over to my desk and sat down in my chair. I leaned back and let out a very loud sigh. I could feel the anxiety kicking in. My heart started to race. I knew I had to do something. I had to get out of there. All those feelings and emotions with everything going on at the time, I just couldn't take it. I debated on what to do, if I should go have a drink or call it day. As I sat there, I finally decided to get up. I walked out in the shop, looking around. I could see Ellis working. I walked over to him.

"Hey man, I'm going to burn out for a little bit. I'll be back."

I saw a confused look on his face. He walked over and asked me where I was going.

"Man, I'm just going to get out of here for a little bit, get from fresh air."

"What's going on, Tyler?"

"Nothing, brother, just gotta clear my head for a little while."

"I saw Anna here. What did she want?"

I didn't know what to tell him. I mean we were close, but normally I didn't talk about those things, and even when we did, I always held back. Sometimes you just can't say what you want to say. Even though I knew I could confide in him and I could trust him not to tell anybody, saying it out loud made it even more real.

"You know I'm always here if you want to talk," he said. "Everything we do, the shady deals and the work we do up here, we're in this together. You can always talk to me. I'm always here. I'm the least judgmental person you will ever meet."

"I know," I said. "It's just that talking about it doesn't change anything."

"I know how you've felt about her all these years. Man, sometimes you just got to let go."

I started to nod my head in agreement. I did agree. It was time for me to let go. I was chasing a unicorn. I was chasing something that didn't exist, and I didn't have the courage to even attempt to do what it would take to find closure.

"Yeah, maybe," I said. "But the heart wants what the heart wants, and no matter what I do, it's not going to change that."

"Well, she's not making it any easier on you coming by here, and it seems like lately it has been more often than not that she comes by here just to say hello. Who knows, man, maybe she is fighting the same battle you are fighting on the inside, but you got to do something. Either you need to walk away or put all your chips in."

I nodded. "Yeah, I think if I could just find a way to walk away that would be the best option." We stared at each other for minute and I said, "Well listen, I'm going to run. I'll be back here in a little while. What time we meeting Eddie?"

"I'll get in touch with him, we'll meet him tonight. Everything is set up."

"Good. Alright man, I will text ya or call ya here in a little while."

I walked out to the car and got in and started it, not knowing where I was going. I pulled out of the shop and decided to head out towards the salt mines. I just remembered I had a couple of Oxys I had put back in my glovebox for a day like today. I started going through downtown Juniper, and was noticing people out. The day was nice. People were out in the streets walking their dogs, just living their peaceful lives. I drove straight through town to about two miles out where I was headed.

As I was driving out of town, I opened up the glovebox and pulled out a pill bottle. There were two Oxys in there, some foil and a straw. I had been saving them for a couple of weeks. I knew today was going to be the day I needed them. I turned the radio up as loud as it would go, and rolled the windows down trying to enjoy the fresh air, trying to get my heart to quit beating so fast. I wanted to clear my head, but I just couldn't. I was consumed by what was going on at this point. I was consumed with her, and thoughts rushing through my head, thoughts of my father and my mother, my brother and my dead brother. I even had thoughts of Lady. Seemed like lately everything was poking its head out at once. I couldn't catch a break. I had lived so long without acknowledging any of these problems, any of these issues that I had to deal with on a daily basis and these past few weeks they were coming to a head. I hadn't thought about my brother in so long. I hadn't thought about him since the last time I really had to detox and I was lying on my bathroom floor—the day I heard the voice. But for some reason, today and these past weeks, I'd been thinking about a lot of things. How I needed to straighten my life up, or at least make it manageable. My business wasn't doing well and I was having to do more and more illegal things to get by. My drug habit had gotten worse, then it would get better, then it would get worse again. It was like a roller coaster, and I realized that this whole trip with me driving out to the abandoned salt mines was to relax and forget all this stuff was just making it worse.

I turned down a long gravel driveway and drove about half a mile before I got to the end, and then it opened up to the salt mines.

The salt mines had kept the town of Juniper booming for years. It had been closed now for about twenty-five years, but there was a point in time when everyone worked there. It was a 'tradition.' It ran in the family, but luckily none of my family had to work there, so even if it would have been open today, I probably wouldn't have any part in it.

As soon as I got to the mine, I drove around to the back and there were several buildings out there. Office buildings and shops, all abandoned and closed and no one ever came down there. Some of the high-schoolers would go down there and drink, and you could tell because there would be beer cans and cigarette butts everywhere. I pulled up to one building. It was the same building I always came to when I went out here. It was towards the back, so not very many people would go in it if they came out here. I had actually set up a chair and there was part of a desk in there against the wall, and it was peaceful. Somebody had smashed out all the windows in this building, so when I went in I could feel the breeze. There was salt mining gear laid on the floor. A hardhat, a couple of tools and several beer cans, and my chair was still there.

I sat down and pulled the pill bottle out of my pocket. I unrolled the foil and laid the first oxy on there. I bent the foil so that it would hold the weight. I put the straw in my mouth, then I heated the foil underneath the oxy with my lighter, and I put my straw about an inch away from the pill, and inhaled as deeply as I could. I then inhaled some more and some more, then stopped, trying to hold it in as long as possible. The taste was horrible, but it was such a reminiscent taste because I knew what was about to come after that. I blew the smoke out. Then I did it again, over and over and over and over as the pill moved down the foil, staining the foil and making zigzag signs in it.

After about the fourth time, I was right where I needed to be. It was a high unlike any other. It was not like heroin where it just consumed you to the point where you would just lay down and pass out, and it was not like taking pills and getting high off that. This was right in between. In my opinion, it was for me, the perfect high.

I leaned back in the chair, and all those thoughts and emotions faded away. I didn't have a problem or care in the world, and that is why I did that, that is why I used drugs. Not just for the physical pain. I used drugs for the mental pain. They were like an instant antidepressant. As soon as they hit your lungs, everything was okay. Nobody ever understood drug addicts, unless they used to be one. There was not a problem in this world drugs couldn't fix. Temporarily, of course. And hell comes along with addiction, but not at that moment.

I leaned back in the chair and I would feel the breeze coming through the broken windows, and I just sat there enjoying the state of bliss. Then, as the high started to fade away, I got the other pill out and started over again. I was never afraid that I would take too much, I would smoke too much, or I would just do too much drugs. That never crossed my mind. Overdosing was something I did not feel like I could do. I had built up such a tolerance that it just didn't scare me. And at the end of the day, so what if I did overdose and died? Then I wouldn't have to deal with this shit ever again.

Those were some of the thoughts that went through my head at that point. I would even catch myself smiling a little bit, but then I started to think about Anna, what I was going to do, what I needed to do. I was too high to come up with a rational decision, but things were a little more clear. If only everything could be this simple. When you were high everything made sense. I sat there for what felt like an eternity, just going over and over in my head what had happened, and then I would switch quickly from Anna to Lady and started to think *could I have a relationship with her?*

Maybe if I put all my effort into Lady, the Anna thing would just fade away. Then, I quickly realized that I would just resent Lady because she wasn't Anna. She was maybe one-tenth as good as Anna, but I knew she would try for me, but it wasn't good enough.

And then, thoughts of my father crept in. Why we couldn't ever get along, why I always felt like when I failed he couldn't wait to tell me all about it. Then, I felt sorry for my mother for having to deal with him. Then, I wondered why I never went and saw my brother in the penitentiary. I pissed and moaned all day long about my problems. I could only imagine what he went through in there, with none of his family writing him or coming to see him. He would write letters and send them out to my mother and father, and I would see them in the trash at times, unopened. They didn't read them. I think my father felt like he got stuck with me, one son in the penitentiary, the other one dead, then I really started to think about my younger brother. He looked up to me so much. He always wanted to do the simplest things in life. He just wanted to have a family, work a shit job and just go home to that everyday, and he admired me because I wanted so much more out of life. I still wanted to dream, even as I'd gotten older I wanted to dream bigger, and then I would think about the times when we were together, talking, and some of our conversations. I guess it had been so long since I really thought about him.

My heart started beating hard again. I was struggling to breathe. I realized I was having an anxiety attack. I had a couple of Xanax. I reached in my pocket and took one of them. I chewed it up. It had a bitter taste, but I had to. Still, after all these thoughts, thoughts that began with Anna were going to end with Anna, because my brother, my mother and my father, Ellis, my business, none of it mattered if couldn't have her. I would tell myself I need to walk away because that was best for me, and it would be what's best, but I think with Anna this was just one of the demons that I would have to fight for the rest of my life. Not being able to have her, that was my baggage that I would have to carry.

I sat up from the chair, started to stretch my legs. I realized I had been there for quite a while. I decided I was going to head home for a little bit before we had to go out that night. I got in the car and for a minute I didn't know if I was going to be able to drive because I was still very high. I felt great, a little depressed, but great. I headed home and pulled into my driveway before I even realized I never turned the radio on. These thoughts were controlling me.

I unlocked my door and went inside. I quickly sat on the couch, lit up a cigarette, and must have passed out. I woke up with the cigarette still in my hand. It had quit burning, and my phone was ringing. I noticed it was dark outside. I grabbed my phone and it was Ellis. He was calling to confirm if I was ready. It was late, so I told him yeah, and I would meet him up at the storage buildings.

Ellis had a friend who rented one of the storage buildings up there, and he borrowed his key and he already had the guns in there. I didn't want Eddie thinking I did any of this out of my own shop. I just wanted to keep those two things separate. As I drove through town, I pulled up to the storage buildings. They were just outside of town, so I felt safe that we weren't going to see any police. There were several buildings, and the one we would be in was towards the back, so as long as we didn't make a racket or have a bunch of lights on I wasn't worried at all. I pulled up and Ellis was already there, had the storage locker open, sitting on the tailgate of his truck. I parked, got out, walked over to him, and sat down next to him.

"What time is he supposed be here?" I asked.

"He ought to be here any minute."

It wasn't ten seconds later I heard a truck pull in, followed by another truck pulling in. I looked back at Ellis and he was looking at me with the same look on his face.

"Shut the door, that may not be them," I said.

He quickly jumped up and shut the door. Then, two trucks pulled up right in front of us. I saw Eddie get out of the first one and there was someone riding with him, somebody I didn't know.

Two other guys I also didn't know got out of the truck behind Eddie. Evidently, they were all together.

I looked over at Ellis. "What the hell is going on?"

He just shook his head. "I don't know."

I knew I had to be cool about this. I needed the cash, and I for sure didn't need the trouble. So, I walked up to Eddie, stuck my hand out.

"Hey man, what's going on?" I said.

He just walked right past me. I was starting to get angry. He was the most disrespectful son-of-a-bitch I knew. He walked straight past me to Ellis, and shook Ellis' hand. Eddie and I never got along. It may be because we were too similar, I don't know. But he was an arrogant loud mouth, I did know that.

I walked over to him and said, "Hey man, this isn't a keg party, what's with all the people?"

He stared at me for a second before he answered.

"I'll bring whoever I want," he said.

"No you won't, not if you want this shit," I said. "I don't want everybody knowing our business. We can load this shit up for you. You don't need them here."

"Those are my boys. They go everywhere I go."

I rolled my eyes and shook my head. "Really dude?"

He didn't respond. I decided not to say anything else after that, not until the cash was in my hand. I couldn't risk it. If I didn't get this payday, I was screwed in a lot of different ways. I wouldn't have money for pills or to pay Ellis. So, instead I just said, "Hey man, they're over here."

We opened the storage building back up, and I pulled the crates out and showed him the guns. They carefully looked over them, and I could tell he was excited about them. Seeing the look on his face was making me regret this deal altogether. I couldn't trust him to get rid of these without my name coming up. If I hadn't been so desperate, I wouldn't have done this. He picked up a crate and was about to put it in the back of his truck.

"Hey man, where's the cash?" I asked.

He stopped and looked at me. He laid the crate on the ground and pulled an envelope out of his pocket and chunked it at me. It hit me in the chest and fell down to the ground. I stared at him and he stared at me. He was trying to piss me off. I reached down and picked up the envelope, and it was thick. I opened it up and I counted it. Surprisingly, it was all there. I put in my pocket. Now it was mine, so I could say and do whatever I wanted.

"Man, next time we do anything like this, you come by yourself," I said. "I don't know any of these people and I don't feel comfortable doing it."

He looked at me for a moment. "Well you know what, I really don't give a shit what you think."

That was the final straw. Ellis could see it. He looked in my eyes. I started after Eddie, got my left hand on his shoulder and turned him around and I reared back about to hit him right in the face, and there was nothing he could do about it. He had that crate of guns in his hands. He was about to just take it, but about that time Ellis grabbed me and yanked me back. Then, Eddie's other friends came charging in but before they could get there Ellis was yelling and hollering and splitting us up, getting in-between us. Eddie was yelling and I was trying to get in his face but Ellis wouldn't let me. Thank God he had a cool head. Because if it would have gotten any further, the cops probably would have showed up. I would have ruined everything, like I am good at.

Ellis pushed me to the side, and then he gave me a real big push and I landed on the hood of my car, and he got in my face. "Dude, let it go. We got what we came for. They got what they came for. Let's lock the storage door and get out of here."

I watched them load the crates up and they were talking in the back of their truck. I don't know if they were planning on what they were going to do with them or what, but I was under the impression that he was getting them out of the state, selling them to somebody else. But then by the way they were arguing and talking, I don't think that was what they were going to do.

I looked at Ellis. "He's getting rid of these quick, right?"

"Yeah, man, he is."

"Look," I pointed at them. "The way they're talking, I think they plan on keeping those things."

Ellis sat there for a minute. He looked at me and I looked back at him. Finally he said, "Nah, surely he'll do what he said and get rid of them."

"We'll see."

I jumped in my car and headed home. I had slept half the day so I knew I wasn't going to go to sleep easy, but I really didn't feel like having a drink. I took a handful of Vicodin, maybe seven or eight of them, so I could really go to sleep, and started my drive home.

CHAPTER 10

About a mile down the road from the storage buildings I pulled over. I realized I was not going to go to sleep anytime soon and it wasn't too terribly late, so I got my cell phone out and called Ellis. I told him to meet me at the shop, I wanted to talk to him. A few minutes later I pulled up and he was already there, waiting on me. I got out of my care, lit up a cigarette and he was sitting on his hood.

"What's up," he said.

"Hey, man, it's not too late. You think you could wait a couple more hours before going home?"

He looked at me with a little bit of concern in his eyes. "Why? What's up?"

"Oh, I don't know, man. It's been a while since we went out and had a decent time. Why don't we go up to the club, have a few drinks?"

"You mean the strip club," he said with a slight grin on his face.

"Yeah, why not? We haven't been in a while."

He hesitated for a minute. "Well, I guess a couple of hours won't hurt. But that's it, just a couple of hours."

"Yeah, man, just a few drinks and that's it. Worst-case scenario, we have a good time."

"No, worst-case scenario is when I get home and my old lady kicks my ass."

I smiled and said, "She's gonna want to do that anyway. At least this way, you will have a good time and you'll deserve the ass kicking."

"All right, but I'm riding with you."

We got in the car and started heading that way. I could tell Ellis wasn't overly-excited about going, that he was just going because he knew I needed him to. I didn't open up and talk much to anybody, but the way things had been going lately, I figured I would bend his ear for a little while. Maybe it would help me feel better.

It wasn't long before he started prying into my business.

"So, what's going on, man? What's been bothering you lately? These past few weeks I can tell something has been on your mind."

I let a few seconds of silence go by, trying to decide how to answer that question. Before I could even say anything, he said, "Is it your dad?"

"Well, I'm sure that is part of it," I said.

"You know, dads are funny. You know your dad loves you, he just has a hard time showing it."

"Yeah, everybody tells me that, but I don't know if I believe it. Ever since the accident, I've felt like I was the one to blame. Every conversation we have ends up in an argument over just about anything. It could be my business, Anna, or even David."

I could tell by the look in his eyes he realized what tomorrow was.

"Man, I forgot, I'm sorry," he said. "Tomorrow would've been David's birthday, wouldn't it?"

"Yeah, it always brings back hurtful memories. You know, I've been to the cemetery every year on his birthday. I don't know why, I don't see the point. It's not like he can hear me, but sometimes it makes me feel better."

Ellis looked at me as if he didn't know what to say, but he started to talk anyway.

"Well, you know, whether he can hear your or not, it's nice to have somewhere to go where you can vent and let things out."

"Yeah, I know."

He changed the subject. "So why don't you tell me what's going on with you and Anna."

"What do you mean?"

"Come on, man. I've known you most of my life. Every time she comes around you're a completely different person. It's like, all of a sudden you're ashamed of all the things you've done and she can see right through you."

"Yeah, but she's married. And even if she wasn't, I don't think that would even matter."

"What do you mean?"

"I mean look at the way I live. It would never be good enough for her. And I don't mean that in a bad way, like she's a snob and I'd have to be a millionaire or anything like that. It's just most of the people in my life that I'm around consistently wind up getting hurt. I bring them down in someway or another."

"We all have our demons, Tyler, we just have to figure out a way to handle and control them."

"Yeah, I know."

"Why don't we change the subject? Why are you wanting to head up there tonight? Is Lady working?"

"Should be. I texted her earlier today and she said she would be working. To be honest with you, I could care less if she was working or not, I just wanted to get out, have a few drinks, have a good time. I don't think a good time is too hard to have in that joint."

We drove a little while longer. We weren't too far away, and we went on to casually talk about the furniture shop, the slight problems he was having with his old lady and what not. As we pulled into the strip club, we parked and got out. Ellis looked over at me.

"I'll tell you what," he said. "Why don't we take a vacation?"

I looked at him for a moment. "What do you mean?"

"Well, I figure we are going to be in there a couple of hours. Let's pretend none of this shit we talked about even exists. Let's just spend the next two hours getting really fucked up and pretending that we don't have a single problem in this world."

I grinned and slapped the hood of my car. "That's the best damn idea I have heard in months."

We started walking towards the front door from the back lot where we'd parked. As we got to the door, we opened it and the girl up front said "Hey Tyler" and told us to go right on in.

Ellis looked at me with a little bit of confusion on his face.

"I guess you come here more than I knew you did."

I laughed and said, "How else do you think I spend my spare time?"

As we walked in, I noticed almost instantly that Lady was with a client in a back corner of the club. She looked pretty busy, so we went and sat down at my normal table and ordered a couple of drinks and shots. By the time the drinks got there, I saw two girls off in the distance talking to Lady, and by the time I finished my shot and was about halfway done with my beer, I noticed them making beeline towards us.

I looked over at Ellis. "Here we go."

They came over and both instantly sat in our laps. One of the girls introduced herself as Sabrina. I couldn't help but notice she had a very striking resemblance to Anna, which at first kind of bothered me, but in a weird way I started to like it.

"Lady told us to show ya'll a good time until she can get free," Sabrina said. "So how 'bout we all go upstairs?"

I looked over at Ellis, and he looked like a kid on Christmas morning. He'd been here once before with me but it was years ago. It was hard to get him out of the house with his current girlfriend he lived with. Before I could even answer, Ellis had already stood up and grabbed the girl by the hand and she was leading him to the upstairs room.

Sabrina looked at me. "How 'bout it?"

"Sure." Who was I to say no?

We walked upstairs past the bouncers, and Sabina whispered something in one their ears. I guess to keep us from having to pay. As we walked upstairs, she pulled out a key and unlocked one of the rooms. It was about a fifteen-by-fifteen-feet-sized room with a black leather couch that wrapped around three sides of the room. The waitress followed us in and we ordered a few drinks. She sat Ellis down a few feet away from me, then I sat down. Ellis' girl was already on his lap making out with him, which was somewhat common in a strip club, but it was very common in a big smoked-glass room. No one could see in, so just about anything could go on.

Sabrina straddled me, and then she whispered in my ear, "We have a surprise for you."

She lay down on the coffee table and then the stripper next to Ellis saw her and did the same. She reached into her bra and pulled out a little small glass container. I knew what it was before she would even have to tell me. They both had one. They unscrewed the top and they began to put white powder just below their navel, and then she looked at me, I looked at her, and then Ellis looked at me.

"What are you waiting for," Sabrina said.

I could tell Ellis was excited. He was more into cocaine than I was. Wasn't exactly my cup of tea, but it had been a while. *Why not* was all I could think to myself.

Ellis leaned over his girl and snorted the line as quickly as he could. "You only live once," he said.

I shook my head knowing I would regret this. I leaned down, closed one nostril and snorted the other line. I came up with a head rush and said, "Well, you can only die once, too."

It only took about two seconds for the cocaine to kick in. I was wired and feeling good. The girls got up, started dancing to the music. Before I knew it, thirty minutes had passed by and the girls were still dancing. They had started to sweat, as had I. I don't know if it was the cocaine or if it was just hot in there. I still couldn't keep my eyes off of Sabrina—the way she looked, the way she acted. She resembled Anna so much. And now that I was even more stoned out of my mind, I could see it more and more. It was almost like she was her evil twin. She physically looked like Anna, but she was the exact opposite, which was kind of nice in a way. After they sat there and danced for another fifteen minutes, Lady came in the room.

"Hey guys, ya'll having fun?"

I was still a little bit out of it, but I could tell Ellis was in his comfort zone. She came in, spoke with Sabrina for a few seconds, and then Sabrina left. Lady sat down beside me.

"So what was that like?"

"Well, it was a little bit different," I said.

"I'm sorry. Alan, one of my regulars, came and he is a very big tipper. When he comes in I kinda have to stop what I'm doing and tend to him. I wish I could've been up here."

"Hey, don't worry about it. It's your job, it's what you gotta do. I just came up here to have a few beers."

She looked at me and I could tell she was frustrated. Maybe even disappointed?

"Oh, is that the only reason why you came up here?"

"Well, among other things," I said. "I guess I did want to see you, too."

"You guess?"

I started to get frustrated. I sighed and said, "Lady, what do you want from me?"

She just stared at me. She wouldn't answer, and I could see ten feet away Ellis was still having a good-ol' time with his girl.

"Maybe we should go downstairs and talk for a while?"

"Hell, we're in a room now, why can't we just talk here? Ellis isn't paying attention. He's in heaven right now. He could care less."

"I just wish there was more between us."

"Lady, we met here, and I have been coming here for years. Everything's fine the way it is. Why does anything have to change?"

"Well, I have been offered another job."

"At another club or what?"

"No. Actually as an office assistant. You know, I could wear nice clothes everyday. I could keep regular hours. And I wouldn't be stripping for money. What do you think?"

I didn't want to tell her the truth. I didn't want to tell her that I wanted her to keep stripping. That I wanted things to stay the same. She was my outlet for my problems, and if she got a regular job and I couldn't come up here, things would definitely change. I knew I was being selfish, but I didn't know what to tell her.

"I don't know, Lady. You should do what you think is best for you."

"Well, what if I was thinking about what's best for us?"

I knew this day would come but it couldn't have picked a worst time. I knew I was going to have to end things with her, simply because it would never work out between us, whether she had a real job or not. And I knew after tonight, nothing was going to be the same.

"Me and Ellis made an agreement before we came in here that we were going to be on vacation the next few hours, so we weren't gonna talk about our problems or anything. We were just going to come in here and have a great time. Can I still do that? And if you still want to talk about this in the morning, we will."

"Fine, I guess."

"Listen, Lady, it has been a crazy few weeks and these next couple of days are gonna be bad, too. I just wanna get through those, so if you can just give me a couple of hours."

"What do you mean these next couple of days are gonna be rough on you?"

"Come on, do we really have to talk about it?"

"No, Tyler, you don't ever talk to me about anything. You come up here, we give some dances, I usually hook you up with some pills, and we go back to your house and have sex. Maybe I need more than that."

"It's been working this way for a while now. Why do things have to change? They're fine the way they are."

"Well they're not fine for me anymore. All I want you to do is open up to me one time."

I put my head down because I knew the only way I was going to get out of this conversation was by telling her something.

"Just tell me. Maybe you will feel better."

"Listen, tomorrow is my brother's birthday."

She looked at me funny. "I didn't even know you had a brother."

"Two, actually. One died a few years ago in a car accident. Tomorrow is his birthday." I could tell she was shocked. "Now you know why I never talk about it. I was in the car with him along with my other brother. He was drunk, he shouldn't have been driving, and we had a car accident. My oldest brother is in jail for vehicular manslaughter, and my other brother died."

"I'm so sorry, I didn't know."

"I know you didn't know. I don't normally share these kinds of things. As a favor to me, can we just get out of here? Go back to my house, like normal?"

She had a sincere look on her face. "Sure. I've only got about an hour left. I'm sure I can leave early. Why don't you meet me out by your car?"

"Tell you what, I've still got to drop Ellis off. Why don't I go ahead and leave, drop him off and you can meet me back at the house?"

"Okay, that's fine."

She got up and left and as much as I hated it, I had to interrupt Ellis during what was probably one of the best times he had had in a while. I tapped him on the shoulder. "Hey man, we gotta go."

"Man, what for?"

"They're fixin' to close in an hour anyway," I said. "You need to get home. I need to take you and drop you off at your car."

"Are you sure?"

"Yeah, man. If you want to ride with me, let's go."

He leaned over and kissed the girl on the cheek then reached in his pocket and gave her a few bucks. I'm not sure what he gave her, but knowing Ellis, it wasn't much. He was kind of a tightwad that way.

We walked out of the club and got in our car.

"Did you have a good time," I said.

"Yeah I did. Would've had a better time if we could have stayed a while longer."

"I know, but you don't need to be out, you're gonna get in trouble anyway.

"Whatever you do, don't tell her we were at the strip club," he said. "She'd kill me."

"If it comes up, I'll just tell her we were drinking at the furniture shop."

The ride back to the shop was quiet. I couldn't tell if he felt guilty for what he had done or he just didn't know how to talk to me. Our relationship had started to grow apart, but he was still always there for me.

I dropped him off at his car. We talked for about ten minutes. I knew I had a little bit of time before Lady got to my house. On the way home, I didn't feel like thinking about anything so I just turned the music up as loud as it would go. I even took the long way so I could smoke a couple of cigarettes. I pulled in my driveway and Lady was sitting on the hood of her car, waiting on me. I got out and shut the door.

"How long have you been waiting?"

"Just a few minutes," she said.

"You could have let yourself in."

"I would've, but I figured you'd be here soon."

We walked inside and I grabbed a couple of beers, popped them open and gave one to her as we sat on the couch. She tried bringing up my brothers again.

"Listen, Lady, I really don't feel like talking about it. It's a sore subject. I know you wish I would open up to you more, I wish I could, but I just don't feel like talking about it tonight."

She looked at me. "That's fine, but you're gonna talk to me eventually."

I looked at her. I didn't want to tell her the truth. I didn't want to tell her that I had opened up to her as much as I was ever going to, and I knew after tonight things would be different forever between us. I put the beer down, grabbed her by the hand and took her into my bedroom. She knew I didn't want to talk anymore. She began to get undressed, as did I, and we got into the bed.

I woke up the next morning to the loud sound of rain pelting my roof. It was a perfect day for rain. The things I had to do today — having to go to the cemetery to visit my brother, it only seemed right that it would be pouring down rain. I got up and made a cup of coffee. It was still pretty early. I had only gotten a couple hours sleep, if that.

As I was drinking my coffee, I reached over to my Vicodin bottle and dumped about eight of them into my hand. At this point, that was about an average amount, but I probably should've taken a few more. I knew the day I had ahead of me. Anything to dull that pain. I took them and sat there drinking coffee.

About that time, I heard Lady get up and go to the bathroom, so I knew she was up. A few minutes passed by, and she came walking in to the living room wearing nothing but my T-shirt from last night.

"Good morning," she said.

"Morning. There is coffee if you want some."

"Sure, that would be great."

She went into the kitchen, made her a cup of coffee and sat down on the couch next to me. I knew this conversation was coming, and somehow I think she knew, too.

"Listen, I think we need to talk."

I glanced over at her. "Is that right?"

"I think I'm gonna take this other job. I want to start doing something respectable. Something maybe one day I can call a career, and be proud of myself."

I nodded my head. "I understand."

"Where does that leave us? Listen, Tyler, I know how we met isn't the perfect scenario, but I want to try, I want to make it work."

"Lady, I—"

"Why do you still call me that? You know my name is Annette. I've told you that a dozen times. But for some reason you always call me lady. That's just my stage name."

"I know what it is, and I call you that because that's what you are."

She looked at me confused.

"I wish things were different," I said. "I wish I could look at you and feel like I could spend the next fifty years of my life with you, and we could grow old together and that we could make it work. But I can't do that."

She looked at me and I could see a tear roll down her cheek.

"I just can't do that, Annette. I can't love you the way you deserve to be loved. You've been great to me, and through the years you've put up with more than any one person should have to, but we were never together, and I can honestly say that I don't think we will ever be together. I'm in love with someone I can't have and everyday I think about that. If I tried to give you my heart, you'd never get all of it. I feel like this has gone on too long as it is, and for that I am so sorry. I wish I could give you everything you ever wanted, but it would be a lie and it would never be real. I've always felt like one day you will meet somebody, and know as much as I care about you, and I do care deeply about you, we could never be together, not fully. I couldn't do it all, and I couldn't do it whole-heartedly."

I didn't know how she would act. I didn't know if she would argue with me or get angry or what, but I think she could tell how sincere I was about what I said.

She drank her coffee, sat there for a few more minutes, sat it down and went into the bedroom and started putting on her clothes. I leaned back, wondering if this was a conversation I would regret for the rest of my life. But I didn't want to risk being with someone knowing I would never truly love them just so I wouldn't have to live alone. I would rather deal with the loneliness rather than deal with breaking someone's heart down the road. Especially not hers, she had been so good to me.

She came back in the room. She had been crying more. I could tell she had wiped it from her eyes. She stood above me when I sat on the couch and tried to smile, but she couldn't do it.

She leaned over and whispered in my ear, "I'm sorry. I wish things were different, too." Then, she kissed me on the cheek and walked out the door.

I heard her get in her car and leave. Part of me was relieved, part of me was sad. Today was my dead brother's birthday and I was hoping that those emotions were clouding my judgment, but I could only hope.

Shortly after she left, I got dressed and headed to the cemetery. It was raining pretty hard. I didn't have an umbrella, so I just wore a hoodie to try to keep somewhat dry. My brother was buried underneath a tree. Maybe there would be some kind of shelter from the rain.

I pulled up and walked about twenty feet to his gravesite. Normally I would bring flowers or something, but today I didn't. I just kneeled down next to him, and knowing he probably couldn't hear me, I decided to talk to him anyway. I'd wrote him a letter, and I took the letter out and began to read it aloud.

Dear David, I can't begin to tell you how awful I feel everyday about what happened. Out of the three of us brothers, if anybody was going to do something with their life, it would have been you. You were so happy all the time. You had so many great ideas, and I know you were gonna get out of this small town. Even though you are my little brother, I always looked up to you and admired you. I felt you were the glue that held us together, and no point in my life did I ever imagine having to live without you, as I've had to do these past years. Not only have I had to live without you, but I've had to live without our older brother, too. I haven't seen him in jail. I haven't visited him at all, and I don't know if it is because I blame him or if it's because I blame myself. He has written me in the past and I have never even opened the letters. I want you to know that I think about you everyday, and I love you and I miss you, and I'm so sorry for what happened. I'm so sorry that I couldn't live a better life to make you proud of me, and I'm so sorry that our parents had to go through what they've gone through. Dad blames me for what happened, and he rightfully should. Maybe I should have done something that night, something different. I'm so, so sorry. I love you very much and I think about you every single day. I don't know if there is a heaven or hell, but if there is a heaven I'm sure you're in it. So please, forgive me. I love you. Always your brother, Tyler.

I took the letter, put it back in the envelope and I leaned it against the grave. At that time, I turned around and my father was standing behind me. There was no telling how much he heard, but he had an umbrella. He walked up and stood beside me. We sat there for a few minutes without saying anything. I dreaded anything he had to say to me, especially in this situation. He looked over at me, and I couldn't tell if he was sad or angry.

"You know, son, a father should never outlive his sons."

I didn't have anything to say to that. There was nothing I could say.

"I've got one son who died and another in jail. I wish you wouldn't constantly try to ruin your life."

I wiped my eyes. My whole face was wet from the rain, and I could feel myself tearing up. I didn't want to argue with my father, not today. I looked over at him. "I'm sorry I disappointed you."

He looked at me and I could tell he wasn't sad anymore, he was frustrated and angry. "You know, I'm sorry, too." He started to walk off.

"Dad, let me ask you something. What could I have possibly done to make you proud of me?"

He didn't turn around for a few seconds. Then he turned around and looked at me. "Anything else."

I began to become angry. I just stared at him eye-to-eye. I wasn't going to break eye contact with him.

"Your mother couldn't make it here today. It was too much for her, and I feel it's probably a good thing she didn't."

"Yeah, you're probably right," I said.

He turned around and walked away. I sat down and leaned up against the tree. I was soaking wet at this point. I sat there for a few minutes just thinking about everything — the accident, and everything that had transpired since.

I reached in my pocket to get a cigarette and when I pulled them out they were soaking wet. I stood up and chunked them against the grave because I was pissed. As I turned to walk away, in the distance I could see someone walking up towards the grave with some flowers and an umbrella. I stopped for a second. As she got closer I could tell it was Anna.

She walked up and said, "Hey, I didn't know if you'd be here today." She leaned down and put the flowers against the grave, picked up my cigarettes that I had thrown and handed them back to me. "You know those things will kill ya."

I half-ass grinned. "Not soon enough, I promise. It's good to see you." I started to walk off and she grabbed me by my arm.

"You're not gonna stay?"

"I've been here long enough."

"I saw your dad walking off."

"Yeah, he was loving and caring as always."

"Tyler, you have got to let that go."

"How can I let it go when it's constantly being thrown in my face?"

"That night was not your fault."

"You weren't there, Anna, you don't understand."

"You weren't driving. It wasn't your fault."

"Yeah, but I could've done something. Maybe I could've driven."

"Well then you'd be in jail."

"Maybe I wouldn't have wrecked."

"You don't know that. You have no idea what God has in store for —"

"Please, Anna, not today, just not today. Don't talk to me about God when I'm standing at my brother's grave when he died so young, and I lost my other brother because he's in prison."

"Why haven't you gone to see him?"

"I don't know. I'm afraid to, I guess. I'm afraid it will just make me feel guiltier."

"Your mom tells me he writes her. Did you know that?"

"No, I didn't."

"You know, he's in a bad place in there. If you think you feel guilty, imagine how he feels. Maybe you should go see him."

I shook my head. "I don't know if I could do that."

"Tyler, it's time for you to start facing the reality of things and start taking responsibility."

I didn't understand, and I was slightly frustrated. "What do you mean?"

"You've got to get a grip on your father, your brother, your mother, and the other thing."

"What other thing?"

She put her head down like she didn't want to say it to my face. She started kicking her feet and messing with her toes like a nervous habit, like a twitch. "The drugs."

I tried to get a few words out, but I didn't know what to say. I tried so hard to keep that from her, to keep that bad part of my life away from her.

"How did...what did you..." I couldn't even get out a full sentence.

"I've known for a while, Tyler. You're not that good at hiding it, not as good as you think you are. The pills, the drinking, and God knows whatever else."

I just didn't have anything to say. I was stunned. She was the only person in this world I didn't want to know.

"How did you find out?" I asked.

"I've always known. And you know how I know."

I looked at her confused. I didn't know what she meant by that.

"I don't know if you know this or not, but I've been there for you."

"Anna, you have a family and a life and you can't be there for me."

I could see her starting to get sad, and the look on her face was a look I hadn't seen in a long time.

"Then, tell me how I have been."

"I don't know. Listen, today is a really bad day. Maybe another time."

"Promise me," she said. "Promise me you'll try."

I walked over and leaned in close and whispered in her ear, "I'm sick of making promises I can't keep."

I kissed her on the cheek and walked off, soaking wet.

CHAPTER 11

I finally looked down at my watch and realized I'd been driving in circles for hours, just thinking, thinking of everything. Thinking about both my brothers, my father, and I was doing a lot of thinking about Anna, too. I didn't know how she knew about my drug problem. I guess it bothered me that she did know, but what was I gonna do, confront her about it or wait for her to confront me about it. She had already tried and I just shrugged it off. I sat there behind the wheel of the car, listening to the rain pelt down on the windshield, thinking about the past and every decision I'd made that got me right here, to this very moment. My business was failing. Every relationship I had was failing. It seemed like every decision I had made was the wrong one, and I didn't have the courage or the balls to fix them, to do what was necessary to make everything right.

Finally, after driving for so long I decided to pull into the bar. It was still pretty early, but I knew I could get a drink. I expected it to be empty this time of day. This town was full of a lot of people that needed to drink, but very seldom at this hour are ever in there drinking.

When I pulled in, I noticed there were a few cars there, but I didn't think much about it. I jumped out of my car, shut the door and ran inside as quick as I could. As I opened the door, I instantly got a big whiff of stale cigarettes and stale beer. I shut the door behind me and took my jacket off and tried to wring out some of the water before I hung it up.

I put my coat on the rack and as I did, I noticed a couple people who had been sitting there were getting up. They were leaving. I was very surprised at who I saw. The first person walking towards the exit was Amy, the girl I went to school with and who worked at the bank. It was odd seeing her here. She wasn't the type. I was sure there was a story behind that.

The next person was no surprise to see. It was the town screw up, Eddie Stevens. He walked behind Amy. He was always in here causing some kind of trouble. I didn't want to talk to him or even have a couple of words with him after selling him those guns. I just wanted to forget it happened and move on with my life.

Both of them slowly walked by me, not even looking up or in any other direction. They just stared straight ahead towards the exit as they walked out the door into the rain. They stood outside for several seconds, getting soaking wet before they each went to their cars. It was very odd seeing them act the way they did. You would've thought they had seen a ghost or somebody had died. But, I had other stuff to think about, so I just quickly shrugged it off.

As I walked up to the bar to find a place to sit, I noticed they were the only two who had been in there at the time. There was not even anybody playing pool or anything. It was just me, and it was kind of nice. The thought of running into somebody I knew and having to have a fake conversation just wasn't really something I could do today.

I grabbed a stool and sat down and around the corner came a man, one I had never seen before. He wasn't any of the normal bartenders or the owner. He was a tall black man with white hair, and he was dressed very differently than what you would usually see in this town. He had a string necklace with what looked like different teeth from different animals on it, along with pieces of bone, and he was wearing what looked like a suede vest, but almost as if he had made it himself. He was very odd. I knew he wasn't from around here. Or if he was he was new. He approached me where I sat.

"What would you like to drink?"

He spoke with a weird accent that sounded like he was from the south, even further south than Juniper. Maybe from the coast, or Louisiana, almost as if he had some southern French accent. I wasn't sure. I told him I wanted a whiskey.

"All right, one whiskey coming up." He reached back behind the bar, poured a whiskey and handed it to me. "Rough day?"

I sighed and said, "Ah, you know, same as the rest. So, you new here? Where are the other bartenders?"

He shrugged. "I'm just filling in for the day."

"Are you from around here?"

"I guess you could say I'm from a lot of different places."

I could tell just by a few questions he wasn't going to answer any of them. Not truthfully, at least. I had gotten that vibe from him. There was a part of him that drew me into him. I don't know if it was his mannerism or the way he carried himself, or even the way he looked at me. Part of me felt like I'd known him my whole life, but I was just meeting him for the first time. But at the same time, part of me was telling me to get as far away from the man as I could. He had long fingernails. Something seemed off, but at the same time, something just seemed perfectly right with him. It was a weird feeling, a feeling that I never felt before. Inside, I was debating on whether or not to leave or stay forever. I didn't grasp what was going on. He could put off a vibe that was very strange, but I shrugged it off. With everything I had going on, none of this mattered. I continued to get small talk from him, but still no solid answers. Very generic answers were all he would give me.

"So what do you do here in this nice little town of Juniper?" he asked.

"You know, whatever I can do to pay the bills. Mainly I have a custom furniture shop I run downtown. I build furniture and restore old furniture."

"Huh, that's nice. Is the business doing good?"

"Some days it is, some days it ain't."

"Well, nowadays seems like everybody's doing what they have to do to make a buck. You're lucky."

I finished off my whiskey, slid it to him and said, "Well, that's one way of lookin' at it."

"Another?" he asked.

"Yeah, go ahead, pour me another one."

As he went behind the bar, he started to pour me another one. "You want ice with this, Tyler?"

"No, man, straight up is fi—" I stopped in the middle of my sentence. He looked at me and I stared at him, which felt like a lifetime, but was really only a second or two. He poured the drink and handed it to me, but I was looking at him. "I never told you my name."

"It's a small town, you know how it is. Everybody knows everybody."

I could tell he was trying to cover his tracks, but he knew my name when I did not tell him.

"No, you're just filling in today, remember? I don't know you. You obviously didn't know me, or at least acted like you didn't know me when I walked in. Now how do you know my name?"

He didn't answer right away, and I was starting to get a really bad feeling. He put both of his hands on the bar right in front of me and leaned his head down and slightly shook it.

"Well, I thought we could talk a little before I started explaining things," he said. "Try to make you feel more comfortable, you see."

"Comfortable for what?"

"See, Tyler, I am just filling in. I came here to see you."

"Okay...to see me for what?"

"Well, that's just it. You're going to have a lot of questions, questions for me that I am not necessarily going to give you the answers to. The only thing I'm going to give you is an opportunity."

The first thing that popped into my head was maybe a job or something illegal or something like that. At no point did I ever think what was about to happen would happen.

"Okay, well I'll tell you what. I am just gonna sit here and enjoy my drink and you try to explain things as best as you can."

He grinned and said, "That's the attitude I like." And when he said that it was almost like his whole personality changed. It's like for the entire time I had been there he had been pretending to be somebody else, and finally he could take the mask off.

"Do you believe in fate, Tyler?"

"To be completely honest with you, these days I don't know what I believe in."

"Well, you see, Tyler, everybody makes decisions every day. You may make a hundred decisions in one day, and no matter how big or how little the decision you make, it changes your life in one way or another. Whether you are at the store and you decide to get twenty dollars in gas or a hundred dollars in gas. You see, if you get less gas you are going to have to stop again, and when you stop again you'll make more decisions, or you don't stop and you won't have any decisions to make. If you decide to take a shower before work instead of after work, well that puts you fifteen minutes behind. So, you may or may not have had a car wreck, or you may have a car wreck because of that."

I was starting to get confused and even a little frustrated. I finished my whiskey and slid it to him, and he instantly filled it back up.

"Have you ever wondered if some of the decisions you made, if you had just made different decisions maybe your whole life would be different?"

"Well, yeah, of course. I think about it all the time."

He slapped his hands together like he was excited.

"I am glad to hear that. People should think that way. You see, you people go around make all these decisions and then you have to live with them. Well, why not think what if? You know Tyler, I can't travel back in time and have you make different decisions. I can't. That is just something I am not capable of doing, or at least I am not willing to do."

I was starting to get annoyed with the man. He was full of shit and I'd had way too rough of a day to deal with it. I stood up from my chair, sat my drink down and said, "Well I'll tell you what, why don't you save this shit for somebody else?"

"No, you're going to sit back down, because you *don't* have a decision here. I am making this decision for you. You see, I'm doing this for a reason. I'm about to give you the biggest gift anybody could have. Like I said, I can't take you back in time and I can't let you re-make decisions and change them, but I am going to give you an opportunity to change your entire life."

I stood there silently. I knew this mostly just had to be bullshit, but at the same time, I was so intrigued and sucked in. His charisma, the way he talked, a small part of me believed him. Or at least wanted to believe him.

"See, Tyler, when you wake up in the morning it's going to be like any regular day. You can go on and do whatever you want. You can go to work, go have a few drinks, go home, go back to bed, it doesn't matter. Or, if you wanted to, you could kill everybody in this town and kill yourself. There's no limit to what you could do. But when the sun rises again, you are going to wake up again on the exact same day, and it will be like it had never happened. It will be erased. Nobody will know what happened. Nobody will be none-the-wiser. Only you will know what you did."

I looked at him, still confused. "So what is the point then?"

"You tell me. You've got one free day to do anything you want to do, any urge you have always wanted to commit to, or any itch you wanted to scratch. Even if you die, you'll wake up like it never happened. But here's the kicker: you only get one day. This is a one-time, once-in-a-lifetime deal. So I suggest you use it wisely."

I was still not impressed. It was a great idea. He must have thought it up and would tell people that and maybe they would go out and do all these things and then have to live with the consequences.

"No, you won't have to live with the consequences."

My jaw kind of dropped. I started thinking *is he reading my mind?*

He put both hands on the counter and leaned up about two inches from my face and said, "Yes, I *can* read your mind."

Okay, at that point I had to admit I was a little impressed. But come on.

"You can't tell me there are things you wouldn't want to do, but are too afraid of the consequences. Questions you want answered, but are afraid of asking them. Hell, you can do anything. Like I said, if you wanted to bungee jump without a cord it wouldn't matter. I am giving you this gift."

"Assuming this was at all true...why me?"

He grinned real big and said "Why, why, why, why? You people always want to know why. Does it matter why? If I said I picked your name out of a hat would that make any difference? If I said I had been following you for years and I wanted it to be you because I felt some kind of connection to you, would it matter? Or if I just said you happened to be the guy walking in here, would it matter?"

"Well, there are billions of people in this world, there has to be a reason you picked me."

"Well I didn't just pick you. You could say I picked this town. The two people you saw walking out of here when you came in, they get the same opportunity. They get the exact same opportunity as you do. They can do whatever they want to do, and it will be erased."

"That sounds nice and all, and as much as I do appreciate the offer, I don't feel like making an ass of myself for a whole day just to wake up and have it all really happened. You are a bartender behind a bar, okay?"

He grinned, leaned over towards me, took in a deep breath and very sternly grabbed both my shoulders and squeezed. He was squeezing hard. I couldn't get away, I couldn't even move for a few seconds. Then all of a sudden there was a flash, and I could see things.

It started out with me and my two brothers as kids, playing in the yard, and Mom coming out yelling at us to wash up for supper. Then it flashed to junior high, the first time I met Anna. Walking in and sitting down and seeing her for the first time, and I could even feel the feelings I felt the first time I saw her. Then a flash to the crash. I was there, I could see the whole thing, when we hit the culvert and when we were flipping in the air, and then the ambulance coming and I could even see me dead brother lying over there, and my other brother crying and screaming. It was so vivid, it wasn't a dream. I was there, I could see it.

And then things started to turn dark, and I could see the darkness turn into light. I was seeing colors that didn't even exist, that couldn't be described because there are no words for them. These were colors that no one had ever seen. There was no possible way they could exist. It was like part of my brain was seeing things in a totally different way. Then, everything started to get dark again, and I could see fire and flames, and inside me I went from being happy with a normal feeling to just this deep dread, this fear. It overcame me. I could feel a single tear roll down my eye, and then another one after it. The emptiness I felt. My life, if it could be described in a feeling was exactly what I was feeling there, a lifetime of wrong decisions.

What felt like several minutes must have been only seconds because he let go, and when he let go he stepped back. I could see it too, something out of him. When I went to stand up my legs were just Jell-O. I fell down to the floor, and I started using my arms, my forearms and my shoulders pulling myself away from him because I was scared. Whatever the man was he was not human. He wasn't normal. He was something else.

The whole time, everything he had been telling me I was certain it was real. That this opportunity for this free day was real. I was sobbing, I was crying, my emotions were going in a hundred different directions. I had never felt anything so strong like that. It was something supernatural. I looked up at him, realizing I wasn't going to get away.

"Are you God or are you the Devil?" I asked.

He started to laugh.

"Well, which one are you?"

"Maybe I am neither, or maybe I am both. Like I said, none of that matters. I just want you to know that tomorrow you get a free day of consequence-free. All these decisions you made that you live with on a daily basis, you have a chance to try to fix them and see how that works. Or if you don't want to do any of that, you might want to go to Vegas and try your luck there, because it doesn't matter. But I must warn you, when you do make decisions and you do these things, they may not have consequences on the day of, but the next day if you make different decisions, those will change things and there will be other consequences. I want you to know that. I did warn you."

Finally, I could get to my feet. "Why, why do I have to do this?"

"You are looking at it as a burden. It is a gift. Use it as you see fit. Like you said, there are billions of people who would give anything for this gift. Now you have it."

I didn't know if I could trust him. Part of me felt like he was good, but part of me felt like he was bad.

"I want you to go enjoy your day tomorrow," he said. "I want you to use it wisely, and maybe I will see you again. And maybe I won't. Just remember, you only get one day."

I stood up and started to walk outside before I bumped into a table. I was still freaked out. I didn't know what was going on, and about that time I reached up and felt my nose was wet. I was bleeding from both nostrils. I'd never had a nose bleed in my life, but whatever he did to me caused something.

105

I jumped in my car and I started it up, not realizing it was already night time. I looked down at my watch. I had been in there for eight hours, but where did the time go? I could swear I had only been in there for maybe forty-five minutes, an hour tops. It didn't matter. I had to get home.

It was still raining outside. I hauled ass as fast as I could to get home, not knowing how in the world I would fall asleep. After everything that had happened, there was no way I could.

I kept thinking about the man, the fact that he was so tall, that he was black and he had white hair, and he had these odd necklaces and the odd accent. Maybe it had something to do with voodoo, I thought. But it couldn't be voodoo, he was either a demon or an angel or something I couldn't figure out. I didn't really see the point in racking my brain too much because there was no way in hell I could ever figure that one out.

I finally pulled into the driveway, got out of my car, and walked inside. I looked at my phone and I had several missed calls and messages. I hadn't gone to work and no one knew where I was. I had two missed calls from Anna and a text message that read *please call me as soon as possible so we can talk*. There was no way I could talk to her right now after what had just happened.

I wondered maybe if I went to sleep, when I woke up maybe it would be like it never happened. Part of me was scared to death, and I wasn't the type of person to be scared of anything.

But then I started to think, what if it was real? And then I realized it was real. When he grabbed me, the things I saw. No human being had ever seen those things. There was no way it could be fake. I could feel it in my heart and my gut and my soul. Everything that man told me and showed me was real.

I did have one free day. I had one free day to do whatever I wanted. Part of me wanted to call one of the other people I saw in the bar and ask them about it, but I didn't see the point. I don't think they would give me any answers, only more questions.

Now, I just had to focus on my free day and what I would use it for. With one completely free day to do whatever I wanted with zero consequences, what would I do?

CHAPTER 12

I woke up the next morning, and I just lay there in bed. The first thing that popped in my head was the events that happened the night before. I was confused, excited, and terrified. While I lay there, all I could think about was if it was real or not, or just some imagination that I had as I was detoxing again, seeing things. I laid there with this small comfort knowing that regardless if it was wrong or not I was going to take advantage of it. Today would be the day that I could change everything. Then I would instantly have doubts about what I was going to do. It was never about how I would use my free day. Maybe I thought about it, thought of all the opportunities and things I could do with it, but every decision that I had made up to that point had all led to this. With that opportunity I had to make the most of it. I lay there for a little while longer. I started to get up, and then that's when I heard his voice.

"Good morning, did you sleep okay?"

I saw the man, the man from the bar. He was in my house sitting on my couch. At first I was startled. I didn't want to show any fear towards him. I didn't want to give him any more of my weaknesses to feed on because I didn't trust him.

Yawning, I asked him, "What the hell are you doing here?"

"I just wanted to remind you of our little talk last night."

I laughed a little bit under my breath. "Do you think that is something you need to remind me of?"

"Well, I just wanted to make sure you understand the severity of the situation." He had a grin on his face with every word he spoke, which was a little unsettling. "How do you feel today?"

As I stood up and walked towards him I realized I did feel different. Something was very off, but in a good way. My shoulders, my back, my knees, nothing hurt. I felt like I had the greatest night's sleep in my life and woke up feeling energized, focused and ready to do anything.

I started to stretch. "What did you do?"

He leaned back on the couch, crossed his legs and said, "I just took away some of your faults. I wanted you focused today. I don't want you to have your mind on drugs or pain or any of those things."

I was still rubbing my shoulder. "So you're telling me I'm not a drug addict, that I don't need pills or liquor?"

"Don't worry, all those ailments will come back, but today and today only you can focus on whatever your true desires are."

I almost wanted to smile because it had been so long since I felt this way. The fog and the depression and everything had been lifted and I could see a future that I would be happy to be a part of.

"What are you?" I asked him again.

"You shouldn't burden yourself with questions like that."

"Okay, then why are you doing this?"

"Again, those are questions that don't need to be answered."

I was starting to get frustrated. "Where I come from people don't do things like this unless there's a price to pay."

He looked at me for a second. "And do you think it's possible that you've already paid that price?"

"No, I haven't paid enough, I promise you."

"Maybe that is your problem. Maybe all you can see is the bad in things. Maybe you should look at this as an opportunity to see the good. Maybe if you could live your life the way you are supposed to you wouldn't need this opportunity at all."

"You know at first I thought you might be God or an angel, but to be honest with you, my gut tells me you're the devil."

He slightly laughed and said, "Think what you want, either way, you have one free day to do whatever you want. No matter what you do today, when you wake up tomorrow it will be like it never happened. You won't have to worry about things, the mistakes you made. You won't wake up in the morning with the agony about the decisions you made and the things you said because it will have never happened."

"Then what's the point?"

"Maybe you just need a push in the right direction."

"Or maybe you're trying to push me in the wrong direction."

He still stared at me. I think he was starting to get frustrated with the fact he couldn't convince me, although he didn't have to convince me. I was going to do what I was going to do no matter what.

When he touched me the night before, I could feel things, things I never felt before and saw things I could never possibly see again, so whether or not he was the devil or God or maybe something completely different that I didn't even know about, he was right. This was a chance for me.

The man stood up. "Now it's your time. You need to go do what you need to do and do it whole-heartedly and don't have any fear, fear for tomorrow."

I turned around and walked towards the bedroom to get some clothes and when I turned back around he was gone. He didn't use the door. He just disappeared. In a weird way it was kind of like insurance for me that he could disappear like that. I felt like the day was real.

I walked into the bathroom and jumped in the shower and my thoughts were once again consumed by something I couldn't control. Part of me wanted to go back to bed, pretend this never happened. Some things in life you're not supposed to know, but the other part of me knew that there was no way I could do that. I needed advice, I needed help, I needed someone to talk to and I didn't have anybody in my life, not with this. I couldn't count on myself to make the right assumptions.

I got out of the shower and got dressed and, out of habit, I walked to the table to make a drink. I grabbed the bottle of vodka but sat it back down, stared at it and realized I didn't even want a drink. I didn't have any anxiety. I didn't have anything, any ailments. I stared at the bottle thinking maybe it would help me out through the day, but I was going to try a day sober. It had been so many years since I had, But a day like today, I didn't want any excuses.

I got into the car and headed to town. I had the whole day so I figured I would go and try to find some advice. I needed some kind of answers. As I was driving through town not knowing where I was going to go, I saw the church, the church that had been there for probably eighty years, the church I had never set foot in. It was a Catholic church. Being the middle of the week, most churches wouldn't have anyone there except for Sundays and Wednesdays. But in the Catholic church there was always somebody there for confession. Of course, I didn't feel like confessing, I just needed guidance.

I drove up to the church parking lot, pulled in, shut off the engine and sat there, and continued to sit there. I went to open up the glovebox to get a few pills, but realized again I didn't need them, it was just a habit. Feeling the way I did today I could learn to live without them. It would be easy.

As I was sitting in the parking lot I realized I had been there for twenty minutes. I knew I was going in, I just didn't know how to say what I needed to say. The only advice I needed to find was what I was going to do if it was okay. I already knew the answer. A married woman is a married woman. Would it be selfish for me to tell her everything, to lay it on the line? Or would it be selfish of me not to? I got out of the car and walked up to the front. I had never been in a Catholic church because around my area there weren't very many of them. You either went to a Baptist, Methodist or a Church of Christ, everything else was wrong, at least in the eyes of the locals.

As I walked in, I immediately felt intimidated. It was a very large church. It was very quiet. There were candles lit and the stained glass alone was so old it was beautiful, then the carvings of Mary and Jesus on the walls. I was impressed. They took their religion serious. There was no one else in there except for a priest. I could see him at the very front. I still hadn't worked up the courage to talk to him so I just sat down in one of the pews in the back. I kneeled down and draped my arms over the pew in front of me and rested my head on the back of the pew. I didn't know what to think, what to say. I needed answers, but I knew deep down I wasn't going to get them and I didn't even understand what I was doing there because there was only one thing for me to do and that was tell Anna how I felt about her, but if this guy was a force of good and he knew what I was going to do, then how would he let that happen? How could that possibly be okay?

As I sat there I began to get nervous, nervous about the decisions I would make and tried to comfort myself by telling myself that none of it would matter anyway. Even though faith is hard to have, I had to have it in the man that gave me the gift. For a brief moment, I started to think about other ways I could use my day. I could talk to my father or my brother. I could write down the lotto numbers. I could do any of those things, but none of them were as high on the list as Anna was. Nowhere near it.

I had been sitting there for about fifteen minutes when the priest walked up.

"You look troubled, son. Is there something you need to get off your chest?"

"Father, to be honest with you I am not catholic."

He smiled back and said, "Well, we can't all be perfect."

I kind of liked him already. In a weird way he gave me a very comforting feeling. He was probably about forty years old, had brown hair with a beard. Strangely, it was almost comical that he looked like Jesus, but I understood it. It did make me feel more comfortable. He said down in the pew in front of me and turned around and started to talk to me.

"So, why did you come here today?"

"You know how it is, Father, all the other churches around here are only open on Sunday."

He grinned. "Fair enough. But what is on your mind?"

"Well Father, I guess what I don't understand is why God would give us these feelings when they are wrong and expect us to deal with them."

"What do you mean?"

"Like if you have the urge to do something and you feel obligated to do it, like it is your purpose here, what if it is a sin? Are you still supposed to do it?"

"Well that is why God gave us free will. He wanted to show us right and wrong and leave it up to us to make the decision."

"Father, I want to cut to the chase here. I am in love with a woman who is married to another man."

"That is a fairly common these days."

"But I don't feel like I can live without her."

"You don't have to as long as you don't cross any boundaries with her."

"That's the problem, Father. I'm an all-or-nothing type of guy. The thought of not having her fully is heart-aching."

"I understand. So what is your dilemma?"

"Do you believe in the devil, Father?"

"Yes, of course I do."

"Well, I don't know if it's the devil tugging at me or if it's something else, but I have today and today alone to tell her how I feel."

"Why only today?"

"It's too complicated," I said. "I couldn't even begin to explain it Here I am sitting and staring at a beautiful church in front of a man who's given his entire life to serve his lord and the only thing I can think about is her. Everything about her is perfect to me. She is the only reason I can imagine I was put here on earth."

"Sometimes we don't know what the Lord's plans are for us."

"I am not really concerned about God's plans. I know that she is the only thing for me. She is the only thing that matters because at the end of the day, if I can't have her then I don't see the point in any of it."

"Does she know how you feel?"

"I am pretty sure she does, Father, but I've never said it out loud. And I know that it's wrong, and I know the chances are I won't end up with her, but even if there is a one-percent chance then I'd sell my soul a thousand times for that. People live every single day and they struggle with purpose and the point of life and I do too, but the only thing I know for sure is that she was put on this earth for me and I was put on this earth for her, and I know it's very complicated and it's hard and I may rot in hell for this, but she's worth it to me. It's so hard being next to her, seeing her, watching her smile and having to hide everything. The only thing I can think of right now is how I want to have her to talk to every night. I want every decision I make to think of her first and how it is going to affect her."

"Well, son, how do you know there's not some other perfect person out there for you?"

"There is. It's her. Like I said, I have doubts about everything in my life, but she isn't one of them. My question for you, father, is can God forgive me?"

He looked at me, pulled his glasses off and started to wipe them down with his robe. He put them back on and said, "Son, God is the most loving thing in this entire universe. He always forgives and he made us in his own image, so don't think he doesn't understand or that he doesn't know the pain you feel."

"Love makes us do crazy things," I said. "But when you love someone enough it is worth risking everything for, even if she doesn't feel the same way. That's the pain I can live with. But the pain I feel every day by living a lie, that I can't do anymore."

"Would you like to step into confession?"

"No, I think I'll come back for that. Maybe tomorrow, I'll have a lot more to confess to."

I stood up and shook his hand. As I was walking back to the car I dropped my keys. I leaned down to pick them up and I looked who was driving past the church. It was Eddie. Then I started to think about the night before and seeing him there and his free day. I started to wonder. Part of me wanted to catch up with him and ask him, but I started to think about my day and I had my own problems to deal with. So, I got in the car and started it up and decided to head to the shop for a minute.

I was on my way to the furniture store when I had this very intense feeling about my free day. I had some time to kill so I decided to head up to the prison to visit my brother. I hadn't seen him for so long. I figured no matter what happened, it would be like it never happened, so I would go visit him for a while.

It was about thirty minutes up the road and I figured I'd change my mind a dozen times before I got there, but once I was in I was in. I pulled up to the gates to the prison, went inside and filled out some paperwork and waited. I had been sitting there about ten minutes when I heard the buzzer go off to let him in. I was nervous. All these years I had gone without speaking to him and I really didn't have a reason. It was an accident, but I was thinking differently today. Not because it was a free day but because I didn't have a foggy mind, I actually cared about things.

The drugs and drinking had consumed me, but I was finally going to get some things off my chest. I still didn't know if I was angry at him or if I felt sad for him, but I knew by the end of the day every problem I had would be resolved.

CHAPTER 13

I was sitting there in the booth, staring across the glass, waiting on my brother. My stomach was tied up in knots. If I'd been anywhere near a bathroom I would've just thrown up. I never imagined I would be this nervous to see my own brother.

It'd been so long since I had seen him, though. I had avoided everything about him and I never knew why. Maybe I needed a few months to recover from the accident. By that time the drugs had sunk into my bones and every decision I made after that was always the wrong one.

I didn't know what to expect. Was he going to be angry, hateful or maybe he would just be happy to see me? With each passing second I was starting think I'd made a mistake, but I was already sitting there and they had already gone to get him, so I knew there was no turning back.

A few more moments passed by and I could see him in the distance as the guards were patting him down. He had changed so much. His hair was long, he hadn't shaved in weeks. I could tell he had a bruise under his eye. He didn't have to say a word, I knew he'd had a rough time in there. I knew I should've been visiting him this whole time. I blamed him for something that wasn't his fault. It was just an accident. We were all to blame that night. We were all acting stupid.

As he approached, I could feel my eyes start to water because I was excited to see him, and I was hating myself for not coming to visit. I was also very scared he wouldn't even want to have a conversation with me. As he got close to the window and realized it was me he stopped dead in his tracks. He stared at me for a few seconds, which felt like a lifetime, and then he sat down in the chair. I had the phone up to my ear ready for him, and he just continued to stare at me. Then I saw one tear fall down his face. He picked up the phone.

"How you doin'?" he said.

"Ah you know, I can't complain." It was hard to even muster up those words. My throat was dry. "So, they treating you okay in here?"

"How's Mom and Dad?"

"Good I guess. You know Dad, he's still an asshole."

"What about Mom?"

"She is doing okay. She still carries the weight of the world on her shoulders." I could see him grinding his teeth, shaking his head.

"You know, neither one of them ever come up here to visit me."

"Yeah, I know."

"Neither have you."

"Yeah, I know that, too."

"So, why you coming now?"

"I don't know. I should've come sooner. I was so angry."

"I know. It was my fault."

I gripped the phone tight and pushed it hard on my ear because I could tell that somehow or another he felt everything was his fault, and this was my opportunity to let him know it wasn't.

"No, brother I wasn't angry at you. I was angry at myself. I was angry because I never came to visit. I was angry because I didn't know how to handle the loss and the way life treats you sometimes."

I could tell he was finally hearing things he wanted to hear. He was starting to cry even more.

"Listen," I said. "That night wasn't your fault. We were all drinking."

"Yeah, but I'm the one who had the accident."

"And that's exactly what it was, an accident. It could've happened to any of us."

"But it's my fault. I killed him."

"No, the accident killed him. I know you feel so alone in here, stuck in your cell with no contact with the outside world, but just so you know, it's the same out there. Our father feels the same about me as he does about you. The only conversations we have is when he is telling me how much of a piece of shit I am. Mom constantly feels like the weight of our brother's death is too much for her to bear, so talking to me is just too much for her to handle. So while you are in here don't think for a second you are alone, 'cause I am outside and I have a hundred-million more things to worry about than you do. I think about you every day, and I know what you are going through in here has got to be horrible. So every time you feel like you are alone, think about me out there, I am alone too. I've done nothing but make mistakes since the accident. I've done the worst kind of things to the best kind of people. There is a special spot in hell for me when I die."

He covered his eyes to cover up his tears since crying in prison probably isn't the best thing to do. He was having a hard time getting out the words.

"What mistakes have you made?" he asked.

I looked at him and was starting to get emotional. I didn't regret coming up here to see him anymore, but I did regret the conversation we were having.

"I've made every kind, brother. If there is a certain type of mistake a man can make I've made it, but I came up here today because today is different. Today is the only day that I cannot make mistakes and that is why I wanted to be here, because I felt like this was going to be the right thing to do. I wanted to apologize and tell you I love you, tell you that all these years I didn't come up here to visit that they were my fault and they were bad decisions on my part and had nothing to do with you. Just like you do every morning, I'm sure I wake up with the exact same thought on my mind. *Why did I do that?* And I just wanted to make sure that you knew that I wasn't angry at you anymore and that I was right here with you. You may not see me every day, but I'm staring at the same walls you are."

After saying that, I could feel a weight being lifted of all the bad decisions and regret I had in my life. I could tell my brother could feel them, too. He just stared at me, crying. The weight of those problems was taking its toll. I knew I couldn't be there much longer.

I stood up and he put his hands against the glass. I touched it and said, "Gotta go. I'll see you again soon," and hung up the phone.

I turned around to walk away but once I got to the door I couldn't look back. I knew I made the right decision by coming up here and seeing him. But these problems I had, for some reason, today they were feeling heavier than usual. I think it was the sobriety. Normally, whenever I had any issue or problem I needed to deal with I would just simply take more pills and drink more beer, but I didn't do that today.

I walked through the door and was headed down the long hallway to go out. I stopped and leaned against the wall and for the very first time in my life I was having a hard time breathing. It took a while for me to catch my breath, and it also took me some time to realize it was an anxiety attack. I had never dealt with one because I always had pills. I was always in an inebriated state of mind. Being sober definitely had its challenges. I didn't see how people did it, how they could function and deal with their problems without having something to take the edge off.

I got my shit together and made my way to the door. I could see my car in the distance and for some reason I thought it would be some sort of a safe haven. My legs were feeling heavy and I was still having trouble breathing, and all I could think about was just getting into the car. I was passing people coming in and out, and all I could think about was there's no way their problems are as big as mine, no way they're staring at the type of day that I was.

Finally, I made it to my car. I opened the car door and sat down. I leaned back and put my hands over my face and let out a scream. I had had too much.

This was the first day I had been sober in so long and I had to deal with so much. All the decisions that I had made in the last few years were all clear-as-day to me. I looked back to every decision I made and I couldn't even imagine why I made those decisions in the first place. And now with twenty-four hours to solve them all, to fix them all and to make things right.

I sat in my car long enough to try to get my bearings, and I realized that wasn't going to happen anytime soon. I opened the car door and threw up. For the life of me, I just couldn't see the benefit of being sober yet. That man said he was giving me a gift but I think he gave me something else. I could've handled this day so much easier if I would've just taken my pills like I normally do.

I looked down at my watch and realized it was already ten a.m. With everything I had to do today, I needed to get started. I just didn't know what to do next. I didn't know if I needed to go visit Anna or if I should go see my father. That way I could tell him how I had felt my entire life. That decision was going to be a hard one to make. I didn't feel like I could leave yet. I wasn't ready. I leaned back in my car and covered my head up with my arm, then that is when I heard it, the coughing sound next to me.

It was him, the stranger from the bar. It scared the hell out of me.

"Oh my God, what the hell do you want now?"

He was grinning from ear to ear. "Can't I just check on you?"

"You are pushing me."

"Oh, no I am not pushing you. I am just checking on you to see how your day is going."

"Why did you do this to me?" I asked.

"Which part?"

"Well first of all, why did you give me a day of being sober?"

"Maybe you needed to learn how things really feel."

"I can think of a lot of things I need to learn, but I swear to you that's not one of them. No one should have this kind of day and this kind of situation."

"I don't know why you are so stressed. None of it matters anyway. Nobody will remember anything."

"But I will."

"Well yes, you will."

"Then everything I do I'll have to live with, the other people may not, but I still have to live with it. So in reality, you tell me there are no consequences, but isn't there?"

I could see a look in his eye of excitement.

"Now you're getting it," he said.

"Explain to me why you picked me."

"We could be here for hours. I could tell you a hundred different reasons and none of them would make any sense to you and you'd still be none-the-wiser, so what does it matter?"

"Because this whole day is harder when I don't understand it."

"I'll never get you people. You feel like to understand everything, everything has to have meaning, purpose. Life is nothing but decisions that we make, or I guess decisions that you make, and I'm giving you the opportunity to not have to live with those decisions, a redo, and still with the whining and constantly asking questions. *Why me, what am I suppose to do, wa-wa-wa!*"

I was a little surprised to hear him say those things. His true colors were starting to show.

"You know what, fine. If that is what you want, screw it, get out of my car."

He grinned again and as I started up my car he was gone. The way he disappeared made me feel like maybe I was imaging everything, but at that point I was too far in. I still had no idea where I was going, but I was definitely going to start heading that way.

I turned on the highway and knew I had about thirty minutes to get back into town so I turned my music up as loud as it would go and rolled my windows down. I was just trying to do anything but think, but of course that wasn't going to happen. I was having a very hard time with things, but the music and the peaceful air coming in would help. I figured I would head back to the shop and start there. I was constantly trying to tell myself that no matter what decision I made it wouldn't make any difference, but this was a chance and opportunity that I couldn't pass up, so I wanted to make the most of it. I knew I was going to talk to Anna no matter what. That was the hardest thing I was having to deal with. I would find out today how she really felt, and I was even questioning my motives because even if she did tell me what I wanted to hear, would it matter? My whole life I doubted who I was and the decisions I had made, and if she would still take me after that, the constant stress and burden of feeling like she was all I had and every decision I made had to be in her best interest, was that something I could deal with?

I was gripping the steering wheel tight and caught myself driving way above the speed limit. I had to tell myself to slow down. That was when it came to me.

It didn't matter. Knowing was the only thing that mattered and even if I did have to change everything about myself and do everything differently for her, it would be worth every single second because you can't live a life and not share it with anybody. Ten seconds of happiness would outweigh a lifetime of guilt.

Of course, happiness with her would be a utopia. In my eyes she was perfect. In my eyes she could do no wrong. I only wish she could see herself the way I did. Her small imperfections were the things I loved most about her. The way she would softly talk and look at her toes because she was insecure. She wouldn't look you in the eyes. Those features were endearing.

The more I thought about her the more comfortable I felt with the decisions I was going to make. I loved her, that was all that mattered. I could die today and as long as I told her that, as long as I could get it off my chest, and as long as I could explain to her how deep my feelings were for her, anything after that wouldn't matter. The next fifty years of my life wouldn't matter.

I think I was focused too much on how things would go if I told her and I should've been more focused on how things would go if I didn't tell her. In my mind, it wouldn't matter if I had the free day or not, today was the end of all of it. I was not going to feel guilty anymore. I wasn't going to blame anyone else. I was going to take responsibility for the things I had done to get me to that point.

I would simply tell Anna I loved her more than I have ever loved anything or anyone else in my entire life and that as long as I lived, I would never love anyone the way I love her.

CHAPTER 14

As I was driving back to the shop, Anna was still the only thing I could think about. I could feel my stomach becoming queasy, my heart was beating fast, and I was quickly becoming a nervous wreck. I pulled the car over. I decided if this was what I was going to do, I needed to get it over with. I didn't know how it was going to go but I knew it was the only thing that mattered to me.

Anna's house wasn't far up the road. I didn't even know if she would be home, but I knew I could find her if she wasn't. Part of me wanted to stop and buy flowers, but that just didn't fit our relationship. I wished the drive to her house was longer so maybe I could prepare what I was going to say to her, or maybe even have a chance to rehearse it, but that was never my thing. I always felt like honesty came when you didn't have time to prepare for it.

As I reached her house, I pulled over across the street. I wanted to sit there for a minute, gather my thoughts, try to stop sweating and make up my mind. I knew I had to tell her. I knew it was something I had regretted not doing my entire life. It was the only regret I felt like I couldn't live with any longer. I should have told her how I felt a long time ago. I always thought there would be more time. I thought about the stranger, the free day he had given me, and deep down part of me wished I didn't even have a free day, that I could do this just once and live with the consequences, whether it be with her or without her. The thought of doing this two days in a row was hard to stomach.

Her car was parked in the driveway. Her kid would be at school and her husband's vehicle wasn't there, so I knew she was home alone. That was the one thing I had going for me. I quickly pulled up into her driveway with every possible emotion running through my mind. My heart felt like it was going to beat out of my chest. I stepped out of my car, and as I did she came walking out her front door. She had a look on her face like she wasn't exactly surprised, but I could tell she wasn't expecting me either. As she came closer to my car, I honestly felt like I was going to have another anxiety attack. Maybe I should have had a drink, but I knew deep down being sober was the best thing I could do.

"Hey. What are you doing?" she asked.

"I was in the neighborhood and thought I'd stop by. What are you up to?"

"Oh, nothing. My husband left this morning to go out of town for a couple of days for work. Just dropped my daughter off at school, she's got a sleepover with a friend tonight."

"Oh?" I said with a slight tone of relief in my voice. I didn't have any excuses now. I had the perfect opportunity. "So what you got going on today?"

"Not much, a few errands to run. What about you?"

"I decided to take the day off. I've got a few things I need to take care of."

"Like what?"

"Well I wanted to come by and talk to you for a minute."

She slowly walked closer. I think she could tell by the tone in my voice and the look in my eyes that I really did have something to say.

"Is your mom and dad okay? What's going on?"

"Oh yeah, they're fine I'm sure. I just wanted to talk to you."

I leaned back against my car because my knees felt like they were about to give away. She stepped even closer. She was only a couple of feet away from me. She kept staring at me, waiting for me to come out with it.

"Okay, what is it then?"

"Well, Anna, I woke up this morning and things felt a little bit different for me."

"What do you mean?"

I found myself stepping away from the car and walking in circles trying not to look her in the eyes because for some reason that was so hard.

"Well, Anna, you know, I want you to know this is hard for me."

"What is?"

"Well, every day I drive by your house and all the time we see each other and you have been a big part of my life for a very, very long time, and I can't stand the fact I haven't come over and told you that. And Anna—"

I paused. The next part was going to be hard, and her reaction could make or break me as a man.

She stood there without saying a thing. She was waiting. Part of me thought she knew what I was going to say, but I wasn't for sure.

"Anna, I want you to know that I have been in love with you since the moment I first saw you."

She didn't say a word at first. It only took her about three seconds to talk, but it felt like three lifetimes.

"Tyler—"

"No, Anna, just wait. I know that there was probably a time in our lives when I could have told you how I felt and every day I wake up wishing I would've, wishing things were different, but they're not. But something *was* different this morning when I woke up. I decided to tell you that I'm in love with you, and I'm not telling you that I love you. I'm telling you that I am madly in love with you. When I lay down at night, you are the very last thing that goes through my mind, and when I wake up in the morning you are the first thing I think of and I think of you about five-hundred times a day. You are the only thing that matters to me, and know this is horrible timing, but I have to tell you that."

"Tyler, why are you doing this to me? Why?"

"I don't have a choice. I don't think you quite understand what I'm telling you. I've always been in love with you. I just never had the courage to say it. I can honestly say you are the only reason I breathe every day. Just knowing you are out there gives me hope about life"

"Tyler, I'm married. I have a daughter. This can't happen, we can't to do this."

"Anna stop, you can't tell me there's not a part of you that feels the same way. It may be a very small part, it may be one percent, but just do me a favor, I want you to think about the small part of you that feels the same way. I want you to hold onto it, I want you to grasp it and don't let it go. Better yet, I want you to feel it. Don't think with your head, think with your heart. I know there is something between us."

"Why now?" she asked. "Why didn't you say something sooner?"

"That thought crosses my mind every single day. All that tells me is at some point, and maybe even now, you did have some type of feelings for me."

"That doesn't matter right now. I took a vow. What kind of person would I be if I went back on my word?"

"Anna, you can't think like that. You can't honestly tell me that you love him so much that he is the one you want to spend the rest of your life with. If you got married too young and you made a bad decision, you don't have to live with that bad decision forever. You've got to quit worrying about what people will think, and quit worrying about what people will say. Just do what makes you happy."

I could tell she was starting to get angry.

"Tyler, you're being very selfish right now. You're not thinking of the situation you're putting me in."

"I know this is horrible for you. I know you have a family you have to think about, and I know if you want to get a divorce how hard that would be on you and everybody around you. I wish I could take that burden away from you, but I can't. You've got to understand, every single day is more painful than the one before simply because you are out there somewhere, anywhere, and it's not with me. I've loved you for so long it has consumed me."

"What about the drugs, Tyler?"

I turned around quickly because I knew that was an inevitable part of the conversation. I sat down.

"I don't know what to tell you. This thing inside of me is like a stray dog. Once you feed it, it never goes away. But I am working on that. I'm sober right now and I promise you, for you, I can clean my act up, I can fix all that. It'll be hard, but I can to it. I am very willing to do it for you."

"Tyler, no, we can't do this. This is ridiculous. You waited too long. I have a daughter and a family now. You should've told me sooner. There's nothing I can do about that."

"You can't tell me you are madly in love with him. You can't sit there and tell me he is everything to you, because I can promise you that you are everything to me. There is nothing in this world I wouldn't do for you, and I just need you to understand that, that I would spend the rest of my life making you happy. That would be my only priority. I would die a thousand times if I thought that would make you happy. There is nothing I wouldn't do."

"We just can't. It's too hard. I would be lying if I said I didn't feel—"

Just then, a loud roar of thunder cracked. We both looked up at the sky, it was about to rain.

"Listen, Anna, it's not a mistake. I can't live without you. All these bad decisions I've made, all the bad choices and all the stupid stuff I've done is probably why I have never been able to be with you, but I will quit everything for you."

She was shaking her head, her eyes were watering. Her hands were on her hips in a look of disapproval. I knew she wasn't happy with me right now, but I truly believed she wasn't happy because of the situation I was putting her in, because she did have feelings for me. She just hated admitting it.

Finally she spoke. "It wouldn't matter if that is what I wanted, like I said before, I took a vow."

It started pouring rain. The rain came fast and heavy but she didn't budge an inch.

"I can't just walk away from everything here," she said.

I was starting to get frustrated.

"Yeah, I know. You have a home and a life. You have everything right here in front of you and believe me, the last thing I want to do is take all that away from you. I want to give you so much more."

"I don't think you're listening, Tyler."

"Yes, I am listening. Trust me, I am all ears. It's you that isn't listening. There is no man on this earth that will ever love you the way that I do. I promise you, this feeling in my chest, it is not normal. I've never felt it with any other woman."

The rain started coming down harder. "Come on," she said. "It's pouring down rain."

As we ran to the house, we were both soaking wet. As I looked at her I realized I had never seen her like that before. Her hair was soaking wet, her clothes were so wet they looked like a second layer of skin outlying every curve of her body.

"Let me get you a towel." She went back to the bathroom and handed one to me. She had one for herself. I started wiping my face off. My shirt was drenched. She saw that and said, "Let me get you something to wear." She came back shortly with a sweatshirt and handed it to me. "I'll put on a pot of coffee, and we can talk."

I continued to wipe off my face and arms and I glanced into the kitchen where she was making the coffee. I took off my shirt and started to dry off. I looked at the sweatshirt and it read *Stanford and Sons*. I knew it was her husband's sweatshirt and for some reason I just refused to wear it. The thought of wearing his clothes made me physically ill and I wasn't going to do it. I chunked it on the couch.

I walked in the living room, looking at everything. I knew she may have feelings for me, maybe not as much as I wanted and maybe I wasn't as good as her husband. Maybe I hadn't done enough. Every negative thought was going through my brain.

As I was walking around I realized I had never been inside her house. This was a first for me. It was a nice house, an old plantation-style home. Very big and very nice. She was a meticulous housekeeper.

Then I started thinking about what I lived in and how in the world I could provide for her. There were pictures all over the walls of her, her husband and her daughter. That's when I realized maybe I was fighting a losing battle. She may have feelings for me, I didn't really know for sure at that point, but I kept trying to explain to her how much I loved her, and she just wouldn't listen. She didn't understand I loved her so much more than her own husband does, and I don't think there was any way I could make her understand. I guess I was putting letters together to make words and words together to make sentences. I was about to give up, realizing maybe I had made the wrong decision.

I looked into the kitchen and that is when I saw Anna's hands trembling as she was pouring the coffee. She was trembling because she was scared. Not of me, she was scared of herself right now, this very situation. I was scared, too, because I had come over here and had confessed my love to her, and she was still not listening.

I don't know how or why, but the first thought that popped into my head was how Japan had trained kamikaze pilots in World War II. They had trained their whole lives just to get in an airplane strapped with a bomb and fly straight into an enemy to do as much damage as they could. They were willing to sacrifice their entire life and everything for that mission.

I grinned, realizing that maybe words weren't enough. Seeing her hands tremble was all I needed to see. If I was going to lose this battle, then I had to do everything I could. I had to sacrifice everything.

I threw the towel down, still without a shirt on, and I walked back into the living room. She sat the coffee down and went back into the kitchen. I followed her and as I stepped closer, she turned and looked at me and could see there was something in my eyes. I gracefully put my hand on the side of her face and leaned in and kissed her. She kissed me for just a second then slowly pushed me back.

"What are you doing?" she asked.

"I could tell you a thousand times in a thousand different ways and you still wouldn't get it because you are just so damn hardheaded. So, I guess I am just going to have to show you."

I picked her up by her hips and sat her on the kitchen counter. I leaned in and started to kiss her again. This time there was no hesitation. She was kissing me back. Every second passing felt like lightning shooting through my body.

This was all I ever wanted in my whole life. Every fear and doubt about Anna had certainly gone away for a few seconds. It was the most passionate kiss I had ever had. I kissed her on the neck and things started to heat up. I stopped for a second and looked at her as she was breathing heavy, her heart about to pound out of her chest.

I looked into her eyes and said, "You're soaking wet. Let's get you out of the clothes."

She just nodded. She was speechless.

I slowly pulled off her shirt, kissing her again, and then she wrapped her legs around my waist. I picked her up and we started down the hallway, knowing this would change my entire life.

Chapter 15

We were in bed, unclothed and under the sheets, silently lying with each other. Anna was draped across me as I was on my back. We lay there in silence, pondering what had just happened, how it would affect our future, and how it would affect us today.

I was waiting for something to come to mind to say to her, but I couldn't help myself but to just enjoy the moment. So many years had built up to this. This was easily going to be the greatest day of my life, and I wasn't even sure if it was real. I was completely okay with coming back tomorrow and doing the same thing, but I was afraid it wouldn't work. I decided to push out all the doubts and all the thoughts aside for now because this was the one time I needed to sit back and enjoy the moment.

About that time, Anna let out a big sigh, almost as if it was a relief , like all that had been building up in her system and she had finally gotten it out. I could see a partial grin on her face and then it would quickly go back to confusion. I was sure the situation wasn't easy on her but it wasn't easy on me, either. We just lay there, feeling each of our heartbeats through our chest. I could've laid there forever, but I knew I couldn't. After several moments of silence, she finally spoke.

"So, what took you so long?"

I grinned and said, "Well, I'm not exactly known for making the right decisions at the right time, but I think it is all going to work itself out."

Her eyes cut toward me. "Yeah, you could've done this a long time ago. It would've been a whole lot easier. Why, why didn't you? What stopped you?"

I let out an easy laugh.

She looked at me with a smirk on her face. "Why are you laughing?"

"Well, I doubt you'll remember this," I said. "But it was the second or third time we went out and we were sitting having dinner in the exact same table at the exact same restaurant we always did, and that's when you for some reason decided to explain to me exactly what you wanted out of a husband. You went down to the very detail including what he did for a living, and I always felt like you were making sure I was on board. I always felt like you were seeing if I was going to be ready for the job."

"I said that?" she asked.

"Like I said, you probably wouldn't remember, but things like that I can't forget. And to be honest with you, it was a pretty intimidating conversation, so I decided I would just work harder. I wanted to be everything for you and I still do. I knew it wouldn't be easy. A few things simply got in the way. Anytime something started in the right direction something negative would hit, and then you ran off and decided to get married."

"You know, it wasn't a decision I just made overnight."

She was laying her head on my chest, and I was simply stroking my fingers through her hair.

"I know it wasn't, and you gotta believe me that whenever I tell you that I wish everything was different, I wish I could've told you sooner, but maybe me telling you here, me telling you now with your daughter and everything, maybe this is how it was supposed to be, maybe this is how it was supposed to work out. I don't believe we make wrong decisions in life, I think we simply make bad choices but they are not wrong. There is no right or wrong choice, there are only the choices we make. So as I am laying here with you in this bed, really at this point it is hard for me to regret anything, not for the way things wound up."

"That's easy for you to say, Tyler."

She dug her head deeper into my chest. I could tell she was thinking, probably about the repercussions of our actions. All the negative things that happened lately. That was the last thing I wanted on her mind. We lay there for another few moments in silence before she spoke.

"Maybe I do regret getting married. You telling that I told you exactly what I wanted out of a husband, even though I don't remember that, it sounds just like me. I always had in my head an exact idea of how a husband would be, how the house would be and even how our kids would have acted. Maybe I was too young and just jumped at the first opportunity to get married and start having a family. But it is so hard thinking about the future, going down this road to the very path that it will lead."

I was glad not to hear regret in her voice about the decision she had made about me. After a few more minutes I realized I could lay there forever. I decided to get up and make a day of it.

"Anna, I want to show you something. Can you skip your errands? There's something I want to show you."

"What is it?"

"I don't want to tell you, I just want to show you."

"I think you showed me a lot today."

"Well the day's not over. I still got plenty more to show you."

She looked up at me and said, "Is that right?" And I just grinned.

"Come on and get up," I said. "We're not gonna lay in bed all day, even through that is exactly what I would love to do."

She slowly got up before stealing the sheet and went to the bathroom to get dressed. I got up, hoping my clothes were dry. I was sure they were by this time. I went down the hall, all the way to the kitchen picking up pieces of my clothes. I put them on one by one. Of course, me being me and being very unknowledgeable about women, I was wondering what was taking her so long to get ready. I sat down on the couch and turned on the television to the local channels. I decided to get up to see what was taking her so long. When I walked around the corner we almost ran into each other.

"I'm ready," she said.

"Okay, just making sure you were all right. It was taking you a while there."

She grinned and slapped me in the chest. "I'm a girl."

We turned around to walk out and when Anna went to turn the TV off she stopped for just a second. All you could see was police cars and caution tape, and the bottom of the TV read: *Bank in Juniper robbed. Robbers killed in high-speed pursuit.*

"Tyler, did you see that?"

I walked up and saw what was going on but it was the last thing I cared to think about. "Huh." I reached over and turned off the TV.

"Hey, we got stuff to do. We're headed in the opposite direction, anyway, so traffic won't bother us."

"Where we going anyway?" she asked.

"You'll see. It's a little place I want to show you."

"What are you showing me?"

"Just be patient," I said. "Who's driving? You or me?"

"I'll drive," she said. "My windows are tinted."

"What, you afraid someone will see us together?"

She quickly turned around. "Yes."

"You know that's going to happen eventually anyway."

"I know it is," she said, "but not today. I've got enough to deal with, I don't want to stress over that, too."

"Fair enough," I said.

We walked out the door and got in her Tahoe. She began to back out of the driveway.

"Take a left," I said. "Head out towards Jessup Creek."

"The bridge?"

"Yeah, head out there."

She looked at me with a funny look on her face.

"Why are we going out there?"

"You'll see. I want to show you something."

As we headed toward Jessup Creek, the silence was abnormal. It was as if we both had so much to say the words couldn't match our feelings. Finally she spoke.

"You said today was different. You woke up this morning and it was different. Why?"

"I don't know," I said. "This morning I woke up and I just had this feeling in the pit of my stomach that the thought of going another day without you at this point was just too much to bear. I'm tired. I'm tired of the way I've been living, the way I've been acting and the things I've had to put up with. I just feel like this was the one thing that I couldn't put up with anymore."

She didn't say anything. She just kept driving. Of course, I couldn't tell her the real reason. For starters she wouldn't believe me. I still didn't believe me and I was there. I witnessed everything. I wasn't sure what was going to happen tomorrow. If I would wake up in her bed or if I'd wake up in mine like it had never happened, but either way I was hell-bent on making sure tomorrow started the same way today did.

As we got closer to the creek I instructed her to pull over to the side of the road. It wasn't an overly busy road, especially not at that time of day, but sometimes it could be busy.

Jessup Creek was just out of town. It was a large bridge and the creek ran directly underneath it. A lot of people spent time fishing there. Sometimes it even flooded.

Anna pulled over and we sat there in her car. It was starting to get warmer outside. It had to have been in the mid-80s. We had run the air conditioner the whole way there.

"Alright, get out, I want to show you."

"Tyler, what are we doing here?"

"I'm fixin' to show you, calm down."

She grinned and got out. We walked down to the bridge. A few cars passed, but not very many. There weren't a whole lot of people in the part of town.

"Okay, I want you to look." I was standing at the end of the bridge and about fifty feet away were two very large black marks. "See those black marks?"

"Yeah, the ones that are barely there?"

"Well, barely there now, but when I made them they were pretty thick."

She didn't look surprised at all. "So those are your black marks?"

"Yes. You see years ago, and when I say years I do mean several years, close to eight years ago, I was driving home from work at the door company. I'd gotten off work and in my infinite wisdom decided to stop somewhere and have a drink. I had taken a few pills, too. On my way home, God decided to let it rain, and when I say rain I don't mean just sprinkles, it was flooding. It was pouring. I came across this bridge and lost control of my truck. I slammed on the brakes but I skidded for what felt like thirty minutes, and ran off into the creek. Now, this horrible behavior of mine led to this almost-horrible accident. My truck ended up in the creek and I had to roll the window down to get out. I jumped out of the truck and had to wade through the water and mud and everything else. That red mud would not get off my clothes. I washed those jeans three times trying to get that red mud out. Finally someone told me just take them to the cleaners."

She grinned, knowing where the story was headed and why I had taken her out here.

"You see, a guy like myself who has never, ever taken a single piece of clothing to the cleaners, well this was kind of odd for me. The thought of bringing my clothes to somebody else to wash and pay them for it."

"That was your first time bringing clothes to the cleaners?"

I smiled as big as I had ever smiled. "Yeah, that was the first time." I could tell she had a confused look on her face.

"But I don't understand," she said. "You came in almost every day after that and we cleaned all your clothes."

"Yes, you did. You see, a couple days after I couldn't get the red dirt stain out of my jeans, I happened to drive up to the cleaners, and I dropped those pants off to get them cleaned and that's when I met you."

She now had a big smile on her face, too. Maybe because she felt like I had remembered everything and it made her feel even more comfortable around me. I think she was starting to see that I did love her.

"See, Anna, after I walked into your cleaners everything changed for me. I couldn't imagine living life without you, even after only seeing you for seconds. You hit me like the biggest freight train in the history of man, and I simply wasn't ready for it. I wasn't ready for you, everything that came along with you. I literally knew within seconds of meeting you that I wanted you to be a part of my life forever. I knew I loved you, that it wasn't some fairy tale. Most people don't believe in those types of things but the feeling and the experience that I left with that day were unexplainable. It never happened to me again, and will never happen to me again. With the drugs and the alcohol and everything I was in the middle of, a horrible accident caused the greatest thing in my life to appear right in front of me. I may not have felt good enough for you and may not have even known you long enough that you would have took me just as I was, but that is what getting older is about, understanding things and seeing them from someone else's perspective. See, I made that mistake once—of not feeling good enough, of not telling you how I felt— even after we went out a few times. I just didn't have it in me. I truly felt like I was going to have one shot and I wanted it to count. I wanted to swing for the fences."

"It's hard for me because I never knew you felt this way," she said. "I had a feeling, but never knew you felt so strongly. It's hard for me to understand how you could feel this way."

I grinned and walked up to her on the side of the road, put both my hands on her cheeks and slightly brushed the hair out of her eyes. I leaned in and spoke softly to her.

"This isn't something I could begin to explain, but it is exactly what it is. I could quote a thousand different philosophers trying to explain it, but it just wouldn't do it justice. The English language is lacking the right words for me to really make you understand."

As I was staring deeply into her soft beautiful eyes, she looked down at her feet. She couldn't see it, but I grinned because I knew that was how she was. I reached over and slightly kissed her on the top of her head.

"Why don't we go back," I said. "Let's get out of here before it starts raining again."

The ride back to her house was a little bit different than the ride there. Even on the way back to the car I had put my arm around her. I was very affectionate. I had to constantly remind myself of the company I was keeping. I had to keep what I said in check. Not like I was pretending to be somebody else, just that I was living to my full potential.

On our way home we found ourselves talking, laughing and even holding hands. I could tell her decision was starting to get easier and easier.

Back at the house, she asked me if I was hungry. It had been several hours since I had eaten. I told her yes, so we sat down at the table. She had sat out some bread and lunchmeat and we had a sandwich.

It was getting dark outside, nighttime was coming quick. We sat there for hours, talking about everything. About our lives without each other. About our lives and how they would look with each other. There wasn't any subject left unspoken. She told me stories about her daughter and the funny things she did, and I told her stories about my father and all the irrational comments he made to me. I think for the first time in a long time she understood why I felt the way I did about my father.

As a whole, the day was perfect. It couldn't have been any better. I looked at my watch and realized it was getting late, very late. She could tell I was about to get up. She put her hand over mine and looked at me. "Just stay."

I didn't even say anything. I just nodded my head.

"Let's go to bed," she said.

We got up and went to her bedroom. It had felt like we had been together for our whole lives. She stretched across me and we fell asleep.

That was the best sleep I had ever gotten in my entire life.

CHAPTER 16

The next morning I awoke. I had a slight grin on my face. Happiness had never come to me this early in the day.

I rubbed my eyes and reached over to grab Anna but only got a handful of sheets. That's when I realized I was lying in my own bed. The stranger had been right, it wasn't real. Well, it was real to me but no one else.

I went over the prior day's events wondering what had happened. Even though it was erased and it was like it had never happened, I still could not help but smile. I had to make sure that it was the same day, so I quickly got out of bed, limped over to the TV and realized the man who had given me the gift of sobriety had also taken it away.

As I got to the couch, I had to fall over from my aches and pains and the withdrawal was setting in. I wanted to throw up, but I had to push past it. I knew I had some Vicodin lying around, but I needed to be clear-headed. I needed to do this today without any stress from anything else. I turned on the TV and as I looked at the date and time, I realized he was right. Everything he had told me was true.

The free day had no consequences, I could have done whatever I wanted yesterday. But today, everything I did was going to count. I leaned back on the couch trying to decide what to do. The first thing that popped in my head was to do everything identical to yesterday, but I was so anxious I couldn't find the nerve to go to jail to see my brother. I felt like that was for me and no one else, and I had gotten what I needed.

I decided to get dressed and head over to Anna's. I knew she was in love with me. I knew I could fix all the wrongs I had ever done. I kept seeing her smile in my mind, and that long breath she let out in relief when we were in bed. At this point I could not imagine being without her. Today was the day my love story would start. I knew it wouldn't be easy, but it would be the most rewarding thing I had ever done.

I looked at my watch. I was going to be early to Anna's but I didn't care. All it meant was more time I would get to spend with her. I couldn't believe that the one thing that I wanted in my entire life could finally be mine. That's when I decided to jump in the car.

As I got into town it was the same thing I saw every day: people walking their separate ways, speeding traffic late for work.

I lit up a cigarette to try to take some of the detox away, to try to relax a little. I had a few Vicodin in the glovebox, and I was really contemplating taking them just to take the edge off, but with the detox came pure emotion and the satisfaction of being able to feel again. It was crippling and painful, but I felt like I needed it because I needed to feel a hundred percent about what I was about to do.

I turned down her street and slowly pulled up towards her house when I saw her husband's car was still in the driveway. I quickly pulled across the street to a safe distance. As soon as I pulled over, my stomach instantly started churning. I realized I was already on pace to screw everything up. I should've went to the jail, but it was too late now. I decided to sit across the street and wait for him to leave and then go in as I had yesterday.

Sitting in the car was more frustrating than I thought it would be. All I could think about was the pain I had to deal with and the withdrawals, but I knew it was only temporary. That was a problem I could figure out later. I was going to deal with the problem at hand first. My excitement could barely be contained. All I could think about was just bursting in the door and kissing her, maybe that would work. I didn't want to have to retrace my steps, but I was going to anyway.

I started going over the conversation from yesterday in my mind, trying to remember exactly what I said. I had been sitting in the car for about thirty minutes, realizing how early I had gotten there. I came so close to just leaving and coming back, but for some reason I decided to sit in the car.

After about my third cigarette I saw her husband come out. He had his bags packed. Anna had told me the truth about the trip. Of course, I never thought she was lying, but that just made my comfort level go up because I knew everything was the same as the day I like to pretend was yesterday.

He got out to the car and put his bags in the trunk. He was about to leave when I saw Anna and her daughter walk out. Seeing her face, I felt like I was seeing it for the first time. It was like I had been dreaming about that face my whole life and today I finally got to see it. She was the most beautiful, perfect person I had ever met, and today I would get to tell her all those things and what my life meant without her and how much my life would mean with her. It was a struggle just to stay in the car, watching her walks towards him. That was when her daughter ran full speed from behind her and jumped up in her father's arms. I could hear them talking, but couldn't make out what they were saying. I couldn't help but notice how Anna's daughter hugged his neck. She latched onto him like she was never going to see him again. It was obvious she loved him so much, even though I hated him without any real reason.

He hated me and had every reason to hate me. He wasn't a bad guy, and the way he looked at his daughter, the way she smiled and they were laughing, I couldn't help but think of ripping that apart because that was exactly what would happen.

He put her down and Anna walked up to him. She had a smile on her face that I had only seen once before when she looked at him. She was happy to be a part of his life, and the way they kissed after years of marriage was still very passionate. She grabbed onto his hand like she didn't want to let it go. The three of them together, they were the exact definition of a happy family.

My stomach was very upset. My knees were starting to get weak and I was sweating profusely. I shouldn't have gotten there so early. Seeing that was going to make everything so hard. There was no way I could break up that family.

Anna loved him. Yeah, she might have loved me too, but the way she loved him was a different kind of love. I felt like our love was pure passion and their love was sensible, it made sense. And the look in her eyes when she looked at him was...I'm not sure I ever saw her look at me that way.

Maybe Anna was in love with the idea of me. Now I was starting to doubt if she was ever in love with me at all. But a thousand thoughts popped into my head as he hugged his daughter again and he kissed his wife goodbye. He got into his car and as he pulled out the driveway, Anna stood there waving goodbye.

I spent my whole life thinking she had gotten stuck with him because she got pregnant. But she loved him, and her daughter would hate me forever if I tore them apart. A deep sadness set in when I realized I should've stayed at home and went at the exact time and followed my steps exactly like they were from the day before.

I watched Anna walk in with her daughter, holding her hand into the perfect house in this perfect town, and I realized Anna did not know how perfect she had it. And, what, was I going to storm in there and rip it all away from her? Try to make her happier, when a large part of me didn't feel like she could be half as happy with me. I wanted to wipe out all the doubts in my mind and tell myself just to go do it, this was exactly what I had been waiting for. This was everything to me, but I couldn't do it. I loved her so much.

Even though I felt like she was the exact reason I was put here on earth, that didn't matter. Even if I could walk up there and take her away from him, did it mean I was supposed to?

I sat there staring at the house. Not only did I have to wait for her daughter to leave before I could go up there, I also knew that I'd already made my mind up that I was going to do this. I don't know if I was afraid of the responsibility or if I truly just didn't think of the hearts I would break and the family I would tear apart just to have what I wanted.

I felt one single tear roll down the cheek of my face. It was the detox mixed with all those emotions. Everything I wanted to feel I realized was a bad idea. All my bad decisions led up to this very moment, and I was supposed to make the right decision today. I knew it was Anna, I knew that was the only decision I had to make. All I had to do was go up there and talk to her and everything would be perfect, but I also knew I had a responsibility to myself and Anna not to do that.

All of the thoughts and emotions were going through my head at that point. I couldn't decide what to do. I knew the right thing to do, but I still didn't know what to do. All I could think about was that little precious girl who I had barely even had a relationship with, barely knew my name, all I could think about was her mother telling her that her daddy wouldn't be home anymore and that I would be the one sleeping in her father's spot in bed.

I knew my emotions would be the death of me one day, but not like that. I never imagined I would be standing at the door of true happiness and wouldn't be able to do it. My brain, the thoughts, the ideas, were everywhere. How to fix this, how to get everything I wanted, make everybody happy, I knew that wasn't going to happen. I knew I'd walked into a minefield. I could turn around and walk away or I could walk through the minefield to get to Anna.

Sadness quickly turned to anger. I had woken up thinking some strange man had given me a free day to help, but then I realized he was never there to help me. I felt like maybe he was the devil or a demon. There was no good in him. He showed me I could have the one thing I wanted, and he knew I wouldn't take it, or maybe he thought I would. Maybe he wanted my life destroyed. Maybe there was no meaning to what he was doing.

I was having a really hard time. I leaned back in the seat, ran my hands and my fingers through my hair, wiping off the sweat from my forehead and let out a loud scream and hit the steering wheel several times out of frustration and anger. I didn't know what to do now. I didn't know how to fix the fucking predicament I was in.

I then realized the path I was about to go on, and what I had to do next. I reached in the glovebox and grabbed about six Vicodin and quickly ate them. I didn't care anymore. There was a warm beer in my cup holder from a few nights before and I chugged it. It was disgusting, but I didn't care. I threw it out the window and gave a last gaze at the house. I was going to watch my happiness as I drove away, but I knew I loved her too much to do that to her. It would be one thing if her life was different. At least now I knew that she did love me, but there was nothing I could do about it.

I started the car up and quickly sped off. The only thoughts in my head were of rage and anger and frustration and all I could think about was that stranger, the man who gave me the free day, the opportunity that made my life a hundred times worse.

I hated him now. I despised him. I wanted him dead. I wanted to watch him bleed out with that shit-eating grin on his face. He knew what he was doing. He knew what I would do. If he was powerful enough to give me a free day, then he was powerful enough to know what was going to happen. I was a broken man, barely hanging on by a thread and he was the knife that cut the thread.

It was all over now. There was no meaning or purpose to what I had done. There was no way to justify what he had done. I needed answers. I needed to know what I was up against here.

The first place I could think of was the bar. I didn't know where else to find him, or even if I could find him. It was almost eleven. Somebody would be there. I shifted down to third gear and accelerated the gas. I was going to get there as fast as I could.

I pulled up to the bar and there were only a couple of cars in the lot. I got out of the car, stormed through the front door and saw a new bartender. He told me they weren't open yet. I scanned the room looking for something, anybody, maybe one of the others, I don't know.

Maybe one of the others who had gotten a free day would know where he was, but he wasn't there and there was no way I could find him. I walked up to the bartender and began describing the man, told him he worked the other night. I didn't even know this bartender, he was somebody new. He looked at me in complete confusion, not knowing anything about what I was saying. He didn't have any answers for me. He told me they didn't open for another hour, but he told me to go ahead and sit down, that I looked like I could use a drink.

I sat down in the chair and he poured me a whiskey. I slammed the shot and as the hot sting hit the back of my throat I was scanning the room, looking for something. Anything.

Looking for answers.

CHAPTER 17

I'd been sitting there for over an hour. I was on my third drink. I was waiting and hoping for any sign of the stranger, anything to give me hope, answers, something to give me some peace. I didn't know if I had made the right decision. I felt like I'd made the wrong one, but normally when I felt that way it was because I'd made the right one. This whole day had been so complicated. I had everything, my hopes, my dreams laid out in front of me. I asked for it, and she said yes. Because I never thought more than three days ahead of time I had to stare at the biggest dilemma of my life.

What did I do wrong? Is not doing anything at all the right decision? Now I was going to have to live with even more regret. I'd been given the chance of a lifetime and threw it all away. I couldn't even look at myself. The anger and hatred was boiling inside me. It was even hard to breathe.

I quickly downed the next glass of whiskey and motioned for the bartender to give me another. I was starting to get pretty drunk. I couldn't imagine what kind of person or what kind of being would allow that to happen.

Was this God? Surely not. Give me the one thing I had always wanted and tear it away? Or maybe that was what I was supposed to do. Bow down to my selfish needs and just take what I wanted, but I couldn't let her or her daughter live with that. It never once occurred to me of the complications and the severity of the decisions that I would've made.

I could only see her. She had blinded me. She was everything I'd ever wanted. And even if it was just for a night, I truly felt happiness. Part of me wanted to just be happy. The other part of me wanted to scream and throw things.

Whoever said ignorance was bliss was a genius. In the back of my mind I never thought I could have her, and now I had this feeling, this emptiness inside me that was like being in a desert and someone pouring you a glass of water and then dropping it in the sand. I knew now what it felt like.

I tasted happiness, joy and purpose all in one single day and it was all ripped away from me, and the worst part about it was that I ripped it out myself. I could have just been selfish, I could've just told her, but it wasn't that easy, it wasn't just my life. I'd never thought about that before. How could I be so selfish to take everything away from her and the only thing I could replace it with was me? I wasn't worth that. There was no way I could do that to her.

The door opened to the bar and someone else walked in. I jerked my head to see, but it wasn't him. Was I being naïve? Did I really think he was going to show up? Whatever this was it was supernatural.

Is it possible he knew I would be looking for him? Maybe that was his plan all along, to teach me a lesson. Maybe that was my penance for the bad things I had done, or maybe it was just sheer bad luck. I didn't know, but I had no intention of stopping until I found out.

Another person soon followed and as the door was opening, I heard sirens blow past the bar. Another minute passed and more sirens passed the bar. The gentleman sat at the bar. He was tall, gray-headed. I assumed he was a regular.

The bartender asked him about the sirens. The man said he heard on his police scanner there was a robbery in progress at the bank downtown.

I continued to drink. All I could think about was Anna and her loving me, and how I could've had her. She could have been mine.

Everything I wanted was right there and now I was sitting in the grossest, nastiest, most disgusting place on earth drinking room-temperature whiskey. The smell of that place was enough to drive a normal man out. Desperation kicked in. I needed a drink. I needed to forget, or maybe I just needed to remember. I wasn't sure.

I heard several more cars pass by and then the door slammed open and another man walked in. I couldn't see him well due to the bright light from outside blocking my vision. He mentioned a shoot-out at the bank, and something about Eddie Stevens.

I thought about the conversation I had with Anna, the things I said, how inspired I was, how nervous and scared I had been and how she spent the whole day with me. I grabbed my glass and about halfway through my second gulp, I remembered the words she said to me about being busy, about running errands, and how she said she was going to the bank. Surely she wasn't there.

Surely Eddie hadn't used his free day to plan a bank robbery.

I slammed my glass down. My chest started to tighten. All the fear in the world was caving in on me. What if she was at the bank? What if she was there right now?

I ran out the door, fumbling for my keys. The bank was several miles away but I knew I had to get there and had to get there fast. I knew the odds were she wasn't there, but I had to make sure.

I jumped in the car, started it as quickly as I could, and began to feel my breath. I was breathing so fast. I was terrified. For the first time in my life I had realized that the decisions I had made could cost somebody their life. And not just anybody, it was the woman I loved. My soul, my purpose, everything in my whole life could be in danger. This could very well be my punishment.

I pushed on the gas as hard as I could. I got on the highway and had to swerve to miss a car that was coming right at me. I headed towards the bank. I was going as fast as I could through each gear. The engine was revving as high as it possibly could. I was going to risk blowing it up.

Going through town, I could see everybody was worried, people were in a panic. I was terrified of what was going to come next. I was terrified of what I may see. The crowed was in the road and the streets were full of cars so I took a back way. I lived there long enough to know how to get around faster.

Turning the corner and seeing everyone outside, hearing the ambulance sirens, it was draining me and my chest was getting tighter. I screamed out loud. I just couldn't get there. I was trying everything but it seemed like the bank was getting further and further away.

None of that mattered now. I just had to focus on one thing and that was getting there. I tried to tell myself that no matter what she wasn't there. We would make it through this. Everything was going to be fine, I had made the right decision.

People were in the road. I honked my horn and yelled for them to get out of the way. Finally, I came up to the T in the road. The bank wasn't much further. I slammed into first gear and drove as fast as I could, hitting every gear with a loud rev of the engine. I could finally see the bank.

There were cop cars and two ambulances surrounding the building. People were everywhere outside. I quickly drove up, trying to get there as fast as I could, slamming on my brakes just short of the crowd. The crowd had to be at least forty people outside.

I couldn't see what they were starting at. I was pushing through the crowed. Finally, when I got to the edge of the crowd and looked, my heart sank, my eyes dropped.

There were several dead or injured. They were getting people out of the bank. The bank must have been full. There were people lying on the ground. There were only two paramedics. There weren't enough people to help everybody. The town was too small.

I quickly ran through the crowd. An officer grabbed me and told me to get back. I pushed him away and looked. There was an elderly woman lying down, she had been shot. There was a man in a tie who looked like he worked at the bank, he was also on the ground. There were so many people lying on the ground. I didn't see Eddie, maybe he was one of the bodies under white blankets.

I couldn't find Anna, either. I looked everywhere. Finally, I saw someone crawling on the ground until she collapsed. It was Anna. She had rolled over and she was breathing fast. She was still trying to crawl, to pull herself away from the bank. I ran up to her. She was bleeding.

It looked like she had been shot more than once and there was blood everywhere. I leaned down towards her and started to cry.

"Anna," I said.

She started to cough. She was coughing blood. I grabbed her and put her head in my lap.

"Everything is going to be okay."

I was trying hard to be strong for her but it was so hard. I wanted to scream and cry.

"Anna, it's going to be fine. I'm here, I'm right here."

She tried to speak but couldn't.

"Everything is going to be fine. I'm here. Listen to me, everything is going to be fine."

I continued to reassure her. She put her hand on my cheek and I could feel the blood from her hand. I could see blood coming out from her mouth and knew that wasn't good. I screamed as loud as I could to get somebody to help me but there wasn't anyone. There were too many people.

"I'm so sorry, Anna, I'm so sorry."

She said something that sounded like, "It's not your fault," but she could barely speak. More blood was starting to come out of her mouth.

"No, Anna, don't talk. Everything is gonna be fine. Somebody is going to come help you, I promise."

"Just in case, there's something—" She started coughing again, blood flying everywhere. She was trying to smile.

"You've never been alone," she said.

"What do you mean?"

At first I thought maybe she was dying and her brain was misfiring. I didn't understand what she was saying.

"Don't worry, Tyler. This isn't the end. You are bigger than this moment."

I stared at her. I realized what she meant. I started to cry. The weight of my tears were so heavy it felt like they were pushing my face down, and the blood was so heavy I couldn't hardly breathe.

I remembered the day I detoxed, how horrible I felt and the voice that comforted me. That voice meant everything to me. That voice got me through the most horrific part of my life. Now I knew it had been her. She had been there. She was the one who got me through it. Those were the exact words she kept whispering in my ear.

I started to cry even more and I begged and I prayed to God, or to the Devil, to anybody willing to help. If they wanted my soul they could have it. Anna didn't deserve this. She needed more.

I looked at her and said, "That was you?"

She was crying too and she nodded. I looked at her and I grabbed her hand.

"Don't you dare die on me," I said. "I love you. I've always loved you because you're the only thing I can't live without. I love you so much."

"I know." That was when her eyes shut.

I screamed again. "Please, somebody help me! She's dying over here, please somebody!"

It felt like years, crying and screaming with her on my lap. There was so much blood. Finally, another paramedic came up. I was screaming and crying and the paramedic ran up to me and grabbed me.

"Sir, let us have her."

"No."

"Sir, please, we need to take her."

They started performing CPR then put her on a stretcher. I just fell back to the ground, staring at the sky, starting to pray again, but this time they were prayers of anger.

I wasn't praying for anything, I wasn't asking any questions, I was angry. Then, just like when I was on the bathroom floor, I prayed for God to let me die, let me go straight to hell because I didn't want to feel anything anymore. The weight was too much. My anger was too much. Everything was too much.

"Please, Father, just let me die. Take my life and save hers."

I had wanted Anna my whole life and I'd had her my whole life, just maybe not the way I wanted her. I was so self-centered and selfish I couldn't see that. I was so busy begging and praying and feeling sorry for myself for not having the time with her that I wanted when she was always mine. She was always right there in front of me.

CHAPTER 18

I rolled out of bed and was very startled. Another nightmare. They had been getting worse.

I was on my hands and knees on the floor. I crawled to the walls to get as far away from the bed as possible. Instinctively, I was being told that was where the bad nightmares were happening.

I leaned up against the wall, breathing heavily, trying to calm myself. It had been almost eight months since the bank robbery and the nightmares had not gotten any better. A full night of sleep was nowadays almost impossible.

I grabbed my shoulder and started rubbing it. I was bending my knees, too. The pain was still there. I hadn't taken any drugs or drank a drop of alcohol since that day before the robbery.

I was finally sober, the one thing I thought I could never do. I thought my life would be so much better without the drugs and the booze, and in some ways it was, but I realized how much I felt things now.

It wasn't like my free day. The pain was still there. I had to take over-the-counter medicine for that. I was clear-headed, but distracted from the pain and the emotions. I had taken drugs for so long and drank for so long I forgot what emotions felt like.

When you are clear-headed, everything comes to you all at once. It had become a ritual every morning, to sit there and try to catch my breath hoping for some form of easement.

I sat there and leaned against the wall with my head in my hands. Every morning I replayed the events. I should've told her how I had felt. But, what was done was done, now I just had to face all my problems. Even with anxiety I didn't want to go to the doctor because I was done taking pills, of any kind. My life had gotten to where it was because of drugs, so now it was time for me to face the music.

I slowly got up and glanced around the room, making sure I hadn't forgotten anything. I was hoping the nightmares would ease once I left. It was time for me to put this town in my rearview. Every time I looked at this town and my room and my house and my parents, there was nothing but pain. It was time for a fresh start.

I had already bought my bus ticket, taken care of everything I needed to, and had sold everything I owned. I was ready to go.

After I got my clothes on I went to the kitchen and took some ibuprofen, acetaminophen and naproxen. I would probably have liver failure anyways from all the over-the-counter medicines I had to overtake. It was still hard.

I glanced over at the bathroom. I could still remember that day, thinking I was alone and that no one could help me, and then realizing that I was never really alone. Anna was always with me.

I could hear snoring. I walked over to the living room and my brother was asleep on the couch. He had been out of jail for about a week. We had finally resolved our differences.

I went to my bedroom and opened the dresser drawer and got out an envelope that had a letter in it I had written the day before to my brother. It simply read: *This is all yours. Good luck.*

I placed it on the table. It had his name on it. I placed the keys to my car on top. I hoped he would take care of everything. He earned them, he had paid for his sins. He could use a fresh start and make use of the place better than I ever had.

I was done. It was time for me to move on, to go somewhere else. Anywhere else.

I picked up my bag, put it over my shoulder and then grabbed my other bag. It wasn't far to the downtown bus station. I guess I could've gotten a ride, but thought I could use the walk.

I went outside. It was cold. It was coming up on the holidays. I couldn't have picked a worse time to leave, but part of me also thought it was the best time to leave. I didn't want to pain myself through another set of holidays, all the loneliness and the desperation.

I started walking towards downtown. Traffic was very light that morning. The air was cold and I quickly put my hood up over my head to cover up the bare skin. I had shaved and gotten a haircut to try to become somewhat presentable. I wanted to start the new beginning with a new everything. I needed to have respect for myself and everything around me. I needed to change everything I did. I was hoping that every step towards town would be a little bit of relief, but it wasn't much.

My footsteps actually felt like they were getting heavier, like I was walking into resistance. I didn't care about right and wrong anymore, I just needed some relief, a break, any form of relaxation. I just wanted to breathe again. I realized my footsteps were getting heavier and I was breathing harder because I was coming up and had to cross the one place I didn't want to cross — Anna's house.

I had thought of her just about every day. She almost died that day and it was my fault. She didn't blame me, of course, but I still felt like it was my fault.

She had been in the hospital for a few months after her injuries and then had to go through physical therapy. She had been at home a few weeks. She was finally getting her life back together.

My footsteps came closer to her house until I was finally right in front of it. I stopped for a second. I could see through the window. I could see her helping her daughter. I could see that she was trying to get back to the way things were before. I could see the frustration in her eyes. I knew it would be hard for her, but she had plenty of people to help her.

Her daughter walked away and she stood up. She almost looked out the window, but she didn't. I saw her comb her long hair behind her ears almost if she was trying to figure something out. She was staring into nothing. I could only imagine what she was going through. She was still so beautiful, so perfect.

I looked back at the driveway, to that day, realizing I once had everything I wanted for one short day, but my own fear had kept me from having it forever. I always liked to pretend it was myself that made the decision, but it was my fear.

I was too scared of having her, being responsible for her and trying to give her a home and trying to do what was right. I thought I couldn't do it. That's why I had the nightmares. I felt like everything she went through was my fault, like I could have stopped it but didn't.

I knew as time passed she would be fine, but she was still having a hard time. I could tell.

She went to the kitchen, put her hands on the sink and put her head down like she was trying to catch her breath. Part of me wanted to go in and tell her everything. Maybe she would think I was crazy, maybe not, I don't know. I hadn't talked to her since that day. I don't know if she was afraid of what she had told me or if maybe I was afraid she didn't remember telling me.

I knew how she felt, and I'm sure she knew how I felt, but it was time to let it go. I wanted to just stand there forever just staring. Her beauty was intoxicating and I wanted to drink it in. Just staring at her made me feel high. But it was now time to leave. I had had my chance, my shot. I had made my mistakes, and I was too far gone. She had her life now.

I started heading back towards the bus station. I stopped to get one more last glance but she had already left the window. Footsteps did start to feel lighter after that, felt almost clean, like everything was being washed away.

It could have been worse, I told myself. She could have died that day. I am just glad I was there. That was at least the one thing I could be happy about. I tried so hard for her my whole life and at least I knew she loved me.

I sat down at the bus station. I was a few minutes early, looking around at the different people waiting on the bus, wondering what their reason for leaving was. Maybe the holidays, maybe a fresh start like me.

I had a long bus ride ahead of me. I had decided to go to Seattle. It was about as far away as I could get from this place while still staying in the country. Figured I could get a fresh start there and maybe find some answers. I wasn't going to find them here, so why not look somewhere else, anywhere else.

When the bus finally pulled up I stayed in my seat, anxiety kicking in. Maybe I was feeling a little bit of regret. I was nervous I was doing the wrong thing, running away from my problems. I quickly reassured myself that I had been over this time and time before. There was no other option for me. This was it. Staying here would just cause more pain, more grief and I couldn't do it. Being here wasn't good for anybody.

I watched everybody get on the bus and I was still sitting there. The bus driver walked up to me.

"You riding this bus?"

"Yeah, guess I am."

He grabbed my bag and put it on the bus. I stood up, waiting until the very last minute, looking around the town trying to get one last soaked-up look in.

I was born and raised there, and I wasn't sure I would ever see it again. I wanted to make sure I couldn't forget it. I didn't want to make the same mistakes in the next place I stopped.

It was important for me to feel that, for me to breathe it in. To know that was the biggest part of my life and leaving it was hard, but it was something I had to do.

After my last look I decided to get on the bus. I took two steps on the bus and that is when I heard the most beautiful words I had ever heard in my entire life.

The two words I had been waiting to hear my entire life, and they were real.

I heard her say, "Tyler, wait."

THE END

THE END

Matthew Eaton was born in Tyler, Texas.

CPSIA information can be obtained
at www.ICGtesting.com
Printed in the USA
LVHW010032280421
685801LV00005B/277